Memo
With
Maya

Clyde Dsouza

Dedicated to E.D.D, as always.

This story would not have been written without the encouragement of my wife. Thank you for the understanding and the unwavering support.

I'd like to thank my editor, Chase Nottingham. I stand guilty of not implementing all his sage advice.

This is a work of fiction. Names, characters, businesses, places, events and incidents are either the products of the author's imagination or used in a fictitious manner. Any resemblance to actual persons, living or dead, or actual events is purely coincidental.

Memories With Maya

Even though this is a work of fiction, every effort has been made to ground it in hard science. The author and publisher assume no responsibility for any errors or omissions. No liability is assumed for damages that may result from the use of information contained within. Trademarks and Copyrights are fully respected and acknowledged as belonging to their rightful owners. Some concepts have been invented and phrases and terminology have been coined by the author and may not be used in any way without prior permission by the author.

"Don't leave home without your Wizer...
It's an ugly world out there."

CHAPTER ONE

I ZOOMED IN AS SHE approached the steps of the bridge, taking voyeuristic pleasure in seeing her pixelated cleavage fill the screen. What was it about those electronic dots that had the power to turn people on? There was nothing real in them, but that never stopped millions of people every day, male and female, from deriving gratification by interacting with those points of light. It must all be down to our perception of reality.

I cursed…

There I was, standing at the edge of the footbridge that connected to the plaza level of the shopping mall. It took a fair bit of fumbling with the brightness controls on the phone to see anything in the sunlight. I leaned over the rusty handrail, watching people's heads bob as they descended the steps. They bumped into each other like malfunctioning droids when they connected with the main street below. The assignment was to record some video footage of the tower under construction at the far end of that street, but my visor was left in the car. I was too lazy to make my way back up the multistory parking lot. The phone would have to do. My thumb worked the zoom slider while I simultaneously tried adjusting focus. In my backpack was my laptop, ready to record a stream of video over an ad hoc network.

“The Enhance Algorithm's not for perving, you know.” It was Krish.

“That's not what I was doing!”

How long had he been there behind me?

“Take this seriously, will you? I need help. I'm up against the best, back home. I've got to–”

“–Hey, guys, what's up?” Maya called out as she climbed the last step to reach us on the bridge's platform. Her hair tied in a high ponytail swung from side to side as she walked up to us.

“Hanging out with voyeur Dan while he's down-blousing his days away...”

“I was not!”

“Gross. Grow up you two,” she said, throwing two of her

The scope was still aimed at the tower. The cranes on top were like fingers of an endoskeleton, contrasting against the orange purple evening sky, reaching out... begging... a reminder of our recession hit times.

A digital overlay augmented the live view with details of the tower showing approximate distance from my location, what the finished height would be, and other mundane info the developer insisted on including. Any gimmick–as they called my hard work–might attract publicity, clients and funds for completion of their project.

I pressed the button labeled "After" on the small touchscreen attached to the scope's tripod and the view came alive with a digital image of what the finished tower would look like, complete with dancing sky-scanning search lights depicting a futuristic Gotham City-esque look. I slowly panned the scope around the building, and the overlay aligned with the angle I was tilting the scope at. Zooming in, however, still needed some work to make the overlay scale properly with the live view. I needed Krish and his brain.

The doorbell rang. Crap!

Maya hated it when the apartment was messy. So did I, but when I got caught up in work, it was inevitable. I surveyed the living room. Half-empty coffee mugs, pizza boxes and clothes strewn on the floor. I hit the "mood" app on my phone, and the lights started to dim, diffusing the mess around the room. I loved how low lighting transformed my unkempt couch into a luxurious and inviting loveseat. The projector screen always crept down at a snail's pace, but I wasn't about to open the door till the mood program was complete. A short burst from the automatic aroma dispenser and lounge music drifting through the speakers signaled I was good to go.

"Maya!... Fuck. Get inside!"

She laughed.

She was standing in a purple bra and jeans. In one hand she had a pizza box, in the other, her T-shirt and a bottle. From her sling bag dangling over her shoulder, the laces of her dance shoes drooped, entangled in a pair of earphones.

"Take your sweet time to open up, and I'll deliver next door instead."

She took a swig from the bottle and then stuck her tongue into my mouth.

"Nice. Drambuie?"

"Uh huh." She nodded.

I savored the aftertaste of the honeyed malt, then took the pizza box from her. I was ravenous. Maya sidestepped my clothes strewn on the floor, avoiding jeans, shirt and socks to make her way to the scope.

I watched her walk.

It was only when she had her shoes off that the slight limp in her step was noticeable. Her literal Achilles' heel was a congenital anomaly. She never allowed it to come in the way of her learning ballet, even when others in her ensemble called her "limperina." Her mother had got custom shoes made for her, and the only time she struggled was when performing with bare feet. Indian classical dance was rather unforgiving that way.

"How was today? Hack your way into any corporate data?" she said, looking into the scope. The setting sun was streaming through, and it silhouetted her lithe figure as she peered into the eyepiece. The visor was on the coffee table. I lay back on the armrest of the couch, wore it and hit record.

"Had a narrow escape. Data mining's getting risky."

"You could go straight, you know."

"Trying to do that. The market slump's not helping... man's gotta make a living," I said. "Hold still. Need a picture of you. Thaaaat's it." She paid no attention and kept fiddling with the focus. I moved closer to her.

"Stop that, you perv," she said, shooing me away with her hand. My head was the director's viewfinder, seeking new angles.

"It's the same boring project." I flipped on the display for her to have a look. "I probably need Krish to help."

"He's coming over?" Her eyes widened and those perfect eyebrows arched.

"That depends..."

She deftly tip-toed over to the couch and picked up a Blue glove with a large glowing LED and slipped her hand in.

"Fine then, I'll just leave. You'll not get any of this." She launched herself at the couch and slid off her jeans in one fluid move. "And take those silly sunglasses off."

She traced her nose and lips with her gloved index finger and pressed her palm to her face, the ribbed surface brushing her skin. The other glove on the coffee-table buzzed to life.

Small rubber protrusions on it rippled and settled back into the surface.

"Kinky! You fixed it?"

"Mmm Hmm. Long Distance is not the same without your touch." I moved closer. "What's his problem with us?" I asked, kneeling beside the couch, caressing the sides of her thighs.

"He doesn't have one. Probably just wants to save me from ruining my life?" she said.

"Yeah. I'm sure you'd be better off with a mail order boy from those newspaper ads your mom keeps reading to you."

She stuck her tongue out at me, brushing my hand away.

"Why the fuck do they call grown assed men boys, in those matrimony ads?" I traced my finger over her taunt midriff.

"You prefer a mama's boy then?"

"They can be weaned off mama's boob. Much harder to wean a guy who prefers sluts... Correct?" she said.

"There's no one besides you, and you know it," I said. "If my tongue's not worshiping you when you're here–" I kissed the insides of her thighs, breathing her sweet, familiar scent, "–then it's my fingers pleasuring you… virtually." I reached for the glove on the side table and slipped my hand into it, turning it on and feeling its silicon finger tips come alive. She bit her lip. The cutest overbite I'd ever seen. She held my hand as the glove met her skin. Goose bumps formed on her thighs.

"I want the real thing. I want you. I'm here now."

"And tomorrow you won't be," I said, taking off the glove. She straightened up on the couch and pulled me to her chest. I pressed closer, hearing her heartbeat, slow and rhythmic. It was almost at the same BPM as the song playing.

"You know, Krish is getting this break back home and we can't afford Dad's treatment..."

"Shhh... I know." I traced her lips with my fingers and pulled her on top of me while kissing her forehead. "I'm gonna miss you."

"Feels nice when you hold me this way," she said. "I don't want us to end." We didn't speak another word. The song changed to a softer tempo... so did the mood.

...

I woke to a sliver of daylight striking my eye through a gap in the curtains. Maya was thoughtful enough to attempt to shut them, but she must have left in a hurry. The half-empty bottle was standing on the floor, testament to a good night. I grabbed my sweatshirt, feeling the chill in the room. I liked central air-conditioning; it preserved the scent of a good time. The scope was still on and warm to the touch. So it worked well for long periods. I had to call Krish over to get the project completed. Work got done faster when we were face to face.

"You been drinking?" Krish asked.

I loved my deep husky voice, the morning after. I wished it would stay that way throughout the day, especially on evenings when I was behind the mic at the club.

“Just a bit,” I said, clearing my throat.

“Everything alright? I'm wrapping up at the lab, have to clear out my cabin and then go help Mom. Are you working on the visor?”

“No! the visor can wait. I need the scope working. It's gonna keep me afloat. I'll have'ta give up my lifestyle if I lose this deal.”

“No, Dan! The scope can wait. This job pays the bills to run the damn machine that keeps him alive.”

“You'll get in. They came to you. They found you, remember?”

“You don't get it do you? In India, intelligence is a commodity. Nothing special about me or my algorithms. I need them. They don't need me.” He hesitated, then said, “If you won't do it for me, do it... for Maya.”

“What! Oh, that's low...that's really low, using her as a bargaining chip.”

“Don't play her, Dan. Don't play her.”

“She's a grown woman! and Maya and I...that's none of your business.”

“She's my sister! Not one of those women you hang out with, at the club.”

He disconnected. I threw the phone at the couch.

...

The chrome faucet over the bathtub caught the overhead halogen spotlights and sparkled. I watched as a mound of bath salts slowly dissolved in the swirling water jet. I took a deep breath… the smell of a good life. I should enjoy it while I could. Mom and Dad had instilled the virtues of independence in me from an early age. Why then should they feel cheated in any way if I left home early to make my life. It was not like I ever asked them for help, ever, even during the rare times I was living on food court leftovers. I sometimes found myself voicing those thoughts in my head *ad infinitum*. Self-validation had a therapeutic effect.

I took off my sweatshirt and walked around the house naked, feeling liberated. The tub was almost filled to the brim when I returned. Warm water embraced me as I eased myself lower, allowing the foam to envelop me till I could hear the tiny soap bubbles pop near my ears. I bit into a square of dark chocolate lying on the side caddy.

My eyes closed and Maya's smiling face was projected in my mind's eye. At times, I wished she were living in with me, but that thought always conflicted with my dependence on independence. Krish and Maya adored their parents, yet I felt it would be Krish who'd have a harder time moving out of their family home. Maya was a little different in her approach to life. Her dream was to complete her classical dance training and open a performing arts school.

He was the one attached to his mom. Not the usual mama's boy, and I figured it was because he took over the responsibility to provide for the family after his dad was being cheated off life, slowly but surely.

An involuntary shudder ran down my back. It might have been the cold air, or it could have been from remembering the one time I visited the hospital with Krish and Maya and saw the appalling state their father was in. No one deserved that. A hardworking father and from what Maya told me… a kind man as well, always giving away part of his modest monthly earnings to a charity that provided food for needy children back in their country. It was ironic, then, for him to be rewarded for his deeds that way. The Jesus Christ Syndrome; I labeled it.

"Why is God doing this to us?" she had pleaded, looking at me through bloodshot eyes, while I held her hands in an attempt to console her in the hospital room. Her dad was coughing blood mixed with bile, a sick shade of blackish green, on the starched white pillowcase.

Krish was holding his mother who was crying. I looked at him, and he turned to me. I looked into his eyes; I heard them. I took Maya out of the room. Maybe that was the day she saw and understood my point of view, the futile ritual of begging for miracles. Almost three months had passed since that day. There was no point reliving the past…

…

Those with no luck, planned. My best plans and ideas were born while I was either in the shower or soaking in a bath. I chose the tub lately, because thinking in the shower only ran up my bills. Was there any long-term commercial prospect for the AR scope in a depressed market? Or would I have to keep living on the edge, dodging data cops, or hoping for a break that would be an ideal mix of getting paid and allowing me do things on my terms?

Maya would be gone soon. Why were the highs in my life only in short bursts... chased almost immediately by longer lows? I didn't do drugs like the rest at the club, but I realized what they meant when they spoke about downers. Heck, at least punters could buy their next high. Mom would have said, "Say a little prayer Dan, everything will work out."

Prayer... panacea for some, placebo to others. I thought of it as an epidural administered through the soul to anesthetize the mind.

My thoughts were interrupted by the distinct bloop bleep bloop of a video call coming from the speakers in the living room Always when I was in the bathroom! It had to be Krish. He hated putting off unfinished work. It was a quality I liked in him. He must have rushed home to get on the call. I fumbled with the phone in my wet hands, to ask for a few minutes, but it buzzed to life. "Maya Calling" popped up on the display.

"What's up? Missed you," I said.

"Me too." There was a hint of mischief in her voice. "You busy or got time for a quickie?"

"You lil nympho," I said, looking down at the turbulence building up in my foamy ocean. "I'm covered in soap."

"Mmm. Let me see."

I switched on the phone's camera and aimed it down the length of the tub. "Switch your camera on too."

"Why? am I better than the porn you watch?"

"Maybe," I said and turned the phone around to wink at her. I got out of the tub, dripping water in a long trail to the living room, walking heel first then toe so I did not slip and lose the moment to an injury. A single button on the remote closed the curtains and rolled the screen down. I placed the phone on a shelf near the projection screen and logged in to the server, my fingers flying over the keys in a flurry. On the other end, Maya was doing the same. The sound of her squeaky chair and keyboard filled my room, followed a few seconds later by chunky pixels of her image forming on my living room wall. I transferred the call to the big screen. There she was in all her raw beauty, life-sized, smiling.

"Mmm mmm," she said.

I followed her eyes traveling down my body. Two soapy puddles had formed on the polished parquet floorboards, one around my legs and another some inches in front. I grinned. "You like?"

"Gimme now." Her voice came over the surround speakers. Almost as if she was in the room, whispering in my ear.

"I thought you were Krish," I said, then realized how weird it sounded.

"Well, whatever gets your motor running!"

"No, I mean he was supposed to call."

"We better hurry," she said, slipping on the tight spandex triangle. I watched her hit the button on the waistband

and a blue LED lit up. Almost instantly the glove on my side-table buzzed and moved. Not bad latency! I picked up the glove and wore it.

She smoothed a wrinkle in the spandex with her bare hand, and the haptic pads at the center of my glove came to life. She smiled and sat on her chair, swiveling around to face her camera. A better angle. I sank back on the couch, feeling the cold leather on my skin. I moved my fingers and a second later, the image on the screen arched up in the chair, and her eyes locked onto mine. She must have placed her camera right on top of her monitor. The call was clear enough to see the rubbery spandex undulate. I watched as I created a camel-toe masterpiece remotely.

Teledildonics was sci-fi only a few years ago, yet there we were, pleasuring each other without physical contact. Her eyes closed.

She was not looking at her screen anymore, only sitting with her head thrown back, chin pointed at the ceiling. I was activating almost all those tiny silicon nubs that covered the inner surface of that marvel of Korean engineering.

I couldn't resist buying it when I first saw it in a shop window on a visit to Seoul... There it was, her hot overbite again. A few moments later, her eyes opened.

"Stand. I wanna see you," she said.

As I stood, she rolled her chair forward, coming closer to the camera. Her lips and open mouth filled the screen in front of me. I groaned. She must have heard it on her speakers... she pushed back and watched, smiling in appreciation.

I removed the glove and collapsed on the couch.

"Flattered?" I said, blowing her a kiss.

She blew one back. "Is this how it's going to be from now on?"

"I wish you weren't leaving," I said.

"Long-distance never works out, Dan. How does this end?"

"It doesn't have to. It worked out fine just now. Does it matter if you're across town or the other side of the world?"

"Is this what our relationship boils down to? Skypesterbation?" She turned away. "This isn't a relationship, it's not real. What happens if you meet someone?"

"I'll be virtually faithful to you."

She lowered her head. I could have kicked myself. I had an unpleasant habit of making poor jokes at the wrong time. Maybe it was some sort of defense. Whatever it was, it ruined the moment. "Sorry," I said.

"It's OK. Catch you later." There was an awkward silence. Then the "Call Ended" message flashed on-screen. We hadn't even said a proper good-bye.

CHAPTER TWO

THANKFULLY, I WASN'T IN the shower or tub when the video display lit up. I'd been expecting Krish's call. It had been a week since they left. Our few sporadic attempts at maintaining a sustained video-conference long distance from India was always an exercise in patience.

A dedicated line had been installed at his home, and even paid for by his new employer. It was up and running. I hit the accept button, and within a couple of seconds, a high-definition image of him sitting on a sun lounger, shades on and the sound of birds chirping, filled my room. He leisurely panned his camera. I was envious: Deep-blue sky, fluffy clouds and foliage. My wall got transformed into a living video painting.

"OK, cut it out. You've made your point."

He laughed. "Did you manage to patch the code in?"

"Yup," I said. "I think we have the scope nailed. Zoom is perfect. I'm tempted to get a more powerful lappy and see if we can go portable with this thing and a visor."

"No need to," he said. "I was pondering the same thing, mobility. I have access to all the gear I need here and talented programmers. Let's see if we can impress the Prof. and get some funding, you and me."

"Funding! I'm all ears! Who is the Prof?"

"Professor Kumar. He's the one I report to. He runs the gig at AYREE."

"Ay-ree?"

"It's how we pronounce it. AIRI–Artificial Intelligence Research Incu–"

"Oh, I geddit. Do you think he'd fund us?" I asked.

"I spoke about your work and ideas on Augmented Reality and the AR visor you have in mind. He thinks AR is a natural and significant progression to our current goals with AI."

"Hmm, so we develop a visor that thinks?" I said.

"Something along those lines," he said, "but let's brainstorm a few creative ideas that have potential for practical applications. He could then approach the board with something tangible."

"Ahh... so a catch. He needs approval?" My enthusiasm ebbed.

"Of course he does. He has authority to sanction grants after clearance from the board."

"How is he? As a person?"

"He's an academic not a business person if that's what you mean. I see genuine commitment in him, to furthering AI, and he's shown a healthy curiosity in my algorithms."

Krish had my interest again. Academics were leagues better than businessmen when it came to grants. If they believed in something, then they were in all the way, as opposed to bean counters who were always breathing down your back looking for instant returns.

"He's well liked by the board because of his loyalty," Krish said. "That's what I heard the first day I was given a tour by one of my programmer buddies here."

"Cool. So you've settled in... made friends already?"

"Well, this is nerd-ville, and we speak the same language."

"Hindi?"

He scowled. "No I meant all speak geek, digitalk, so making friends is easy."

"Awesome. Let's flesh things out. I'm in desperate need of funding, or I'll have to downgrade my lifestyle."

He smiled, taking off his sunglasses and turning the camera. "Say hi."

My heart skipped one. Maya! She was standing in the doorway of their terrace in a pair of denim hot-pants and a T-shirt. She waved and shouted to him, "Coffee?"

"Chai latte please!"

She waved, turned into the doorway, and was gone.

"Did you realize we've been talking this long without pixelation or stutter?"

"Yeah." I said. The sides of my lips curved into a smile that I had to arrest. Maya and I could have an exciting long distance relationship, and in high-definition.

...

I'd been indoors for a good straight week, or so it seemed, caught up with perfecting the scope, and the experiments with Krish. It was normal that I did not venture outside the apartment when immersed knee deep in work. Tuna sandwiches and a well-stocked fridge and bar was all the sustenance I needed. As I lay on the floor with my legs up on the sofa, Maya hijacked my thoughts. I missed her. Between her and getting my work in order, I'd put my social life on hold. It had been a long day, and the apartment was stuffy. I craved human company. I was feeling lazy, and it was almost five p.m. A good start would be a much-needed shave and a shower. The kitchen sink was piled high with plates and coffee mugs, and I was running low on clothes. By the time I was finished with chores and personal hygiene, it was 7:30 p.m. and dark outside.

The elevator ride down to the basement was a long one on weekends. I didn't know any people who entered. It looked like everyone had week-end plans. Some smiled at me as if we had met before. I had a thing with faces...I couldn't for the life of me recognize people if we'd met only a few times. There had to be something really distinctive about their features for my brain to place them. I always smiled back, playing along, hoping they didn't bring up some topic that would catch me out.

I approached my car. Damn! It wouldn't start. I'd left the overhead light on and the battery had drained out. Auto-Plus breakdown assistance always took their sweet time to arrive, despite me springing for their gold package. I suppose platinum were the privileged ones. I phoned them, and they promised they'd come around in thirty minutes. Sure they would on a weekend!

There was no point riding the elevator back to the apartment. I kept the car door open and fished out my tablet from my backpack. I killed time sorting tracks and built a playlist for my session. An hour later, I was on my way to The Studio, the city's newest nightspot and a magnet for the who's who. Then again, every new nightclub had its moment in the spotlight when it opened. Locking-in the crowd was the challenge after the novelty wore out. I was good at audience interaction. It was a perfect barter. I got to be in the DJ cabin, away from the common crowd on the floor, free food and alcohol, a bit of flirting, and occasionally even paid. It was not going to be a paid night I was told by James, the resident DJ.

"Mon! Where the hell have you been de past week?" he said, murdering the Jamaican accent, which he admitted he hadn't perfected.

"Don't ask! Under self-imposed house arrest, working."

We high-fived a hello. He put his headset on–one ear encased within the headphone's cushioned cup, the other cup twisted around facing outward so he could cue and beat match his track for a smooth mix. There was a sizable crowd already in the club, a small place with two levels. A huge projection screen occupied a whole wall, and directly below, the wooden dance floor was set on a rubber base. The floor let you feel the bass enter your body through your feet and reverberate inside once the night was underway. James fogged the club and hit the lasers. Cloudy tunnels of green formed as the laser went through its routine.

"What's the plan tonight?" I asked.

"Same ole, same ole... score a MILF maybe," he said, lighting a cigarette. James liked them married. He took perverse pleasure in knowing he was doing somebody's woman. The complications if any, and the satisfaction of well... satisfying an unsatisfied woman, was what did it for him.

He was 27 and never found any woman under 35 interesting. Would I be the same as him in two years? I found it flattering if an older woman eyed me at the club. Then again, I never could guess if it was me or the pedestal–the DJ cabin–they wanted to mount. Climbing into the cabin was a privilege, after all.

The nights when Jenny, The Studio's guest DJ was at the

turntables, were even better. There would be females and males hanging on the cabin door. It was difficult to know if a guy wanted Jenny, or he was sizing you. It was worse when girls came up to the cabin and looked right through you. I noticed how they locked on her fingers while she spun a record; she'd tease the grooves on the vinyl with her finger as she slowed or sped up the pitch. She was not interested in women. A petite five-two, she had thick corkscrew curls. Jenny's perky assets were enticing creamy mounds encased in her trademark suede leather bustier that reminded me of a laced up waffle cone.

I had introduced Krish to her. He would've had a nice time, if he hadn't been such a sissy. She liked nerdy looking guys, finding it fun to call the shots with them, she said. We had slept together once, or was it twice? We were too drunk. After that stint, we remained buddies, helping each other to the fodder on the floor. But that was before Maya. Why the hell was I thinking of Jenny?

"Is Jenn coming in?" I asked, looking up at James while I struggled with a flashlight under the deck table trying to plug in my laptop.

"Keep it in your pants, dude. You hit a rough spot with Maya?"

"Maya's been gone a week now–but that's not the point," I said, before he could throw in another wisecrack.

"Oh ho! So young Dan got de blue balls." There was that tortured Jamaican accent again.

"I was only asking," I said.

"You need a plan B, dude."

"What's that supposed to mean?"

"You know, out of sight…" he said. "You think Maya's thinkin' of you on a Saturday night, out there?"

James got distracted before I could counter him. His gaze went to the bar near the cabin. Sitting on a bar-stool at the center of bar was a woman. She looked about forty. He could spot a married woman in distress, like a shark could smell a bleeding victim. Only in his case, it was not water but the fruity, moist air of the fog machine that carried her scent to his nostrils.

"I suppose she's up for slaughter tonight?" I asked, following his gaze.

"Primo rump f'sure, but the night's just begun. We'll see."

"How do you know? I mean, how can you be sure?"

"What her?... Dat's easy, dude. The rock she's wearing is like a fookin' mirror-ball on her finger."

"So?"

"So she's knowingly or unknowingly announcin' she's married but on de market. She's been sitting at de bar wit no one for the past fifteen minutes."

James went into mentor mode. When he wasn't working on his accent, I guess he pictured himself a bartender on some exotic tropical island. "No guy takes so long in de loo."

"Huh?"

"If she was with someone, he'd be back by now, or he don't care 'bout her enuff!" He went on. "She's also sitting with empty stools to de left and to de right–keeping options open y'know, so she can turn either way, dependin'."

"Maybe she's a hooker?" I offered.

"No way. A hooker by now, would be on the stool next to the joe at the end," he said, pointing to a flabby man partly obscured by the fog. Every time one of the colored lights scanned him, a nice specular highlight bounced off the top of his balding head. "He looks like he can afford de price. Why'd a hooker let him slip by?"

Just as James completed his sentence, the woman looked directly at us. Had the music stopped? I could hear it playing. James nudged me with his elbow. "She's eyeballing you mon!" He poked me in the ribs. "Go on, you haven't had any in a while. This one's on me."

"Generous of you, but I'm not interested," I said, turning away.

"Fuck, you blushing? Ladies and gentlemen… Danny boy is blushing." James was on the mic. People on the floor looked up frowning at the interruption, shook their heads and looked away. The woman at the bar smiled. The tempo had picked up. James asked me to play a few tracks while he worked his way to the bar. The stools were full. He squeezed between the woman and a guy who was probably still trying to play cool or gather his wits to talk her up. The guy was too late… I almost heard the *Jaws* theme playing on a tuba. The display on the CD player said the current track would run out in thirty seconds.

I browsed through my playlist, and with my finger on

the touchscreen of my tablet, I wound up to speed an R&B track. Pinching the spinning animated record on the surface of the tablet, I matched the beat to the current track. I loved the tactile feel of a real vinyl record on a turntable, but the club's wheels of steel had malfunctioned within two weeks of being installed, so it was fake digital turntables and MP3 music for the night.

"Can we have some hip-hop?"

"Too late hunny."

I didn't look up as I eased the fader, bringing in the cued track onto the floor. It was good timing. The final seconds of the previous ran out.

"Nice mix," she said.

I looked up. Wow. Just Wow! We were about the same age, I guessed, though she looked much younger. A swath of her gelled hair came across her cheek and reached her mouth. It looked like she was wearing a headset. She was chewing the corner of her lip, smiling. She had short hair with copper highlights visible around her nape… and those almond eyes. The ring of LED lights that illuminated the cabin from overhead reflected in her pupils. Nice catch-light. The comic book geek in me almost said, "anime girl." She saw me staring blankly at her.

"You're new here?"

"Umm yeah, so is the club," I said.

She laughed. "Yeah, I know, but I haven't seen you, and I've been here since opening night."

"I'm a friend of James, the resident." I said. "I do guest

slots, mostly weekends."

"Nice to meet you..." She held out her hand.

"Daniel–Dan." I held her hand. Soft, cold and wet.

"Sorry!" she said pulling back, realizing it was wet from holding a frosted cocktail glass. I smiled and offered her some tissues. She dabbed her hands with them and wrapped them around the glass.

"I'm Kelly."

"Cool, Kelly, you with someone?" Those words just poured right out. I seriously needed a stopper. She laughed, and I heard her sweet and clear, over the music.

"A bit direct, Dan."

"I meant–"

"It's OK. I'm with some girl friends... Ladies night tonight.

"Are you in tomorrow?" she asked.

"I guess, yeah." It almost sounded like a date.

"Nice," she said.

"Heya, Kelly."

"Hi, James." Kelly winked at him.

James opened the door to the cabin and ushered in his latest conquest. "Dan meet Emma."

I didn't really pay attention to what he was saying except for getting her name. He was interrupting! I shook her outstretched hand and turned around. Kelly was gone.

"Smooth dude," he said, drawing out the "oo." Getting it on with the Boss's daughter. You got game." He picked up the 'phones and moved his hands to the back of Emma's neck, smoothing her hair away, putting the headset on her.

"Kelly's father is the–"

"Yeah, her daddy owns the place," he said.

That was interesting… very interesting.

…

Saturday night at The Studio was always muggy on the dance floor. Those who could not handle the mass of bodies, peeled and made their way toward the left corner of the club where there was air. Two women sat on the "groove rider" near the dance floor. It was an invention by accident. The groove rider was a large sub-woofer that delivered the LFE and much of the lower bass frequencies to the floor. One day, James was sitting on a section of foam left on top of the woofer, and he felt the vibration and wobble as I was playing with the LFO modulator in the equipment rack.

"Christ," he said, "this is orgasmic, mon. Don't stop!"

I leaned over the cabin door, and it took me a few seconds to figure out what he meant. I grinned. "Like this?" I said, turning up the LFO controls. I ran through the oscillator range.

"Yeah, right there, baby," he said. "Feels better than a Brazilian hickey."

"Hmm…" we said together, as the potential of our discovery dawned on us. We got custom foam pads made in the shape of bicycle seats, upholstered them in leather and installed them over the low profile of the sub-woofer. The groove rider was born. It proved an instant hit with some women. We knew we were onto something from the way women shifted around looking for a snug fit of the saddle between their legs. James and I would make a beeline to operate the controls. Some of the more popular mixes produced at The Studio owed their success to the secret LFE track, inaudible but deeply penetrating.

One of the perks of being in the DJ cabin was the supply of oxygen and the luxury of space. The night was muggy at The Studio. Drops of condensation were trickling down the glass pane of the cabin. James was with a forty-five-ish looking woman. She ordered the most expensive drinks on the menu for herself and us. He had tried to shout out her name to me over the music, but I hadn't thought it important. Her blue Curacao based cocktail glowed with an almost neon hue. The drink was spiked with taurine and laced with a layer of black vodka. The goblet carried the club's signature monogrammed cocktail stirrer, a classic fashion statement drink at The Studio. It was an announcement to the crowd that the person holding it had money.

"I dropped my cocktail stick," she said. She ran her tongue over her upper lip deliberately.

"Here, use mine," I said.

I didn't like the minty taste of blue curacao and wanted to get rid of the pretentious drink sitting on the cabin ledge in full view of the floor.

"No, thanks," she said. "I'll use James's."

With a pout and her eyes locked onto his, she slid her

hands down his jeans and disappeared into the darkness below. James was sure to goof up his mix. He reached out for a record. The player was finally fixed, and then his fingers trembled as he tried to put the needle on the groove. He winked at me. “It takes practice,” he said, as he stabilized his hand by resting his wrist on the turntable.

“I'm sure it's hard–”

“No...” He wore a sly grin. “The hard part is keeping a straight face throughout and counting bpm. “Nirvana is when you can mix business with pleasure.” There he was, murdering cliches along with the accent, while mentoring.

“Spare me the–”

“Shit! Kelly's headed this way. Take care of her, Dan.”

“There's a rule against women in here?” I asked.

“Women no. BJ, yes!” He bared his teeth at me. “Handle her.”

Below, I heard a groan and a muffled voice trying to say something. “You'll have to tell her not to speak with her mouth full.” I said, not able to resist his predicament. I turned around and saw Kelly wave at me from the floor. She had left her group of friends and was making her way to the cabin. How was I to stop the boss's daughter from entering? She missed a step and reached out at the last minute to grab at the door for support. I caught her hand.

“Pleased to see you miss.” I kissed the back of the hand. I looked at her face. She had a silly but cute grin plastered on.

“Thank you, kind sir. I'm sure the pleasure's yours. May I come in?”

"Uhmm..." was all I could come up with. I leaned over the thick, heavy, door. About six inches of wood stood between us. I knew it was the alcohol, but she was not drunk, only tipsy. Without warning, I reached for the back of her head and pulled her to me. Beer, then the sweetness of her lip-gloss came through as I sucked on her lip to get rid of the malt taste. What the fuck was I doing? I'd probably get kicked out. Behind me, I heard a shaky bumpy mix come over the club's speakers.

James was not invincible after all.

Kelly must have felt my lips curling into a smile. She held my face as she trailed off the kiss. "Thanks for sharing your pleasure," she said, glassy eyed. She turned around, blew a kiss and walked back down onto the floor. James was recovering from his bad mix. He let me take over the tables and leaned forward, gripping the edge of the mixing desk with both his hands for support, giving in to unfinished business. I took the record from him and cued up the remix of "Satisfaction." I raised the fader on the mixer, and the crowd on the floor roared. It was a popular track.

"Shout yeah! If your DJ satisfies you," I typed on the laptop and hit the send key. The big screen in the club flashed the words.

The crowd roared, "Yeah!"

"If you can't get any... ask @James." I hit the send key again, and the projection screen lit up in bold yellow text. Within seconds the in-box on my phone started filling in with messages. "@James Ring mah bell 2nite baby!" was the first one in.

I got my cue for the next track. Disco with a phat beat was making a comeback. I turned on live streaming, and the text flashed up on the screen. The words bounced in sync to the beat and the bass line. The crowd roared again, masking James's groan coming over the live mic.

"I'm still not satisfied @Dan." It had to be from Kelly. I glanced over at the floor. She beckoned. James nudged me to go on. Ms. Cocktail Stirrer rose, leaned on him and took a long swig from her glass. Expensive mouthwash.

I opened the door and descended into the mass of bodies. Someone in Kelly's group came up with the idea of mixing all their drinks into a beer pitcher. They had everything in there from tequila shots to wine. One of them offered the concoction to me.

"Wait." Kelly took the mug from my hands and took a big sip. She passed it to the girl next to her, then locked both hands to the side of my head and pressed her mouth to mine. I sputtered, but kept my mouth on hers as she squirted the liquid down my throat. The group cheered.

"You should be here every weekend," one guy said.

"Yeah, Dan, how 'bout it?" Kelly said. She pulled me closer and whispered, "How 'bout I talk to Daddy. You also get the boss's daughter after hours." She bit my earlobe.

"Drink up, Dan," someone said. The rest chanted something incomprehensible while I drained the rest of the pitcher.

"What's your plan later?" I asked her.

"They're driving me to the airport. Flying out to join my Mom and Dad for a few days," she said.
I breathed a sigh of relief. I wouldn't be cheating on Maya.

...

Drinking and driving is advice that's never followed, yet people feel it's their duty to offer it *ad nauseam*. I shut my eyes, hoping to focus and invoke some sort of inner power to clear the alcohol out of my system. It never really worked, but every time I was a bit drunk, I did it anyway. I hated not being in complete control of all my senses all the time. I gripped the steering wheel at the last second to reclaim the lane I was skidding out of. It was a good thing the car's ABS kicked in.

Maybe Krish had a point. We needed artificial intelligence after all, an AI to override the brain's misguided definition of what a good time was. Sundays would be a lot better for many who lacked will power, if there was such an AI pill to pop in every Saturday night.

I turned in to the basement and had to wait a while to tailgate a car. I groaned as I lifted myself out of the bucket seat, bumping my head on the low roof of the car. At well past three a.m., the elevator ride to the top of the building was a joy. My elevator rescuer got out at floor eleven. I was riding solo and about to step out on my floor, when the phone rang. Who could it be at that hour? Maybe Kelly missed her flight? Both excitement and guilt returned. The keys to my door dropped from my hand. I leaned my back against the elevator door. The keys could wait. My priority was answering the phone. I fumbled to pull it out of my pocket, my finger hitting the answer key by reflex.

"Where you been, stranger?"

Maya!

"Uh, was at the club. Now home." My voice betrayed my attempt at trying to sound sober.

"Put your camera on. I'm sure some bitch is with you."

"Alone, baby." I said, turning to look at my face in the elevator mirror. As I suspected: Shitfaced drunk. I shut my eyes tight again, attempting to clear my head. It worked at times. "What you doing up. What time is it?" I asked.

"I'd gone out too with Krish and his friends."

"Krish's nerdy friends go out?"

"Well, there was this one guy, Arjun. Didn't look like a nerd to me... Anyway, I can't get sleep... Horny."

"Mmmm magic word," I said, picking up the keys and rushing to open the door. "Gimme a minute to boot up."

"Don't take too long," she said.

The alcohol heightened the pleasure as I saw her larger than life image on the wall. I sat on the carpet on the floor, my back resting on the couch. I slipped on my glove. She wasn't wearing her spandex, just her glove. My head flopped back on the couch, giving in to her expert ministration.

"I should record the glove," I said.

"For action replays when I'm not around? - Kinky!"

"Yeah, your touch stream...don't know when we meet next."

She lifted her index finger and traced it down her forehead, down to her lips and then brushed her fingers across her cheeks. I moved my own gloved covered hand to my face, feeling her touch me. She blew me a kiss and slowly moved her hand lower.

"Gentle. Make it last..." she whispered.

I heard her groan. I looked at her through blurry eyes, experiencing slow dizzy pleasure. My head was a vinyl record spinning down, signaling the end of a happy drunken night at the club. She was resting her ear on her shoulder, her hair covering her face. She was biting her lip. The edge of her lip…

Kelly!

I let myself go, hoping against hope that I hadn't said it out loud. Maya groaned, her voice filling the room. Her right hand gripped the arm of her chair.

…

It was Thursday, and I was marginally behind schedule on the project. Thanks to dividing my time between the nightclub and–who was I kidding?–it was all because of Kelly. Her face kept floating in front of me as I worked. The creepy thing was I didn't ever remember having dreams that I could recall in detail, yet lately, I found myself having them almost every night. Dreams where it was evident it was supposed to be Maya, only it was Maya with Kelly's short hair and almond eyes I recalled the next morning.

Kinky but dangerous.

My phone buzzed in my pocket. I looked at the screen and disconnected the call.

I sent back a text message. “Tied up, honey.”

“To the bedpost I'm sure,” was Maya's reply.

“I wish. I'd send you a photo if I were.”

...

I had to prepare for the presentation ahead, and I was fortunate to have someone like Krish who's second language was coding. My ideas, and his prowess created a fertile ground to breed innovation. We had access to AYREE's infrastructure: programming talent, finance and hardware. Those programmers were code junkies. They were cranking out revisions and enhancements at least twice a day. We decided to meet on the grounds of the AYREE Campus. Krish, the Prof. and another well dressed man who looked about the same age as the Prof. but wearing a turban, were walking on the lawns of the campus. Krish was holding a Tablet PC in his outstretched arms, scouring the grounds. They approached a shaded area with four benches. As they were about to sit, my voice came through the tablet's speaker. “I'm on your far right.”

Krish and the Prof. turned, scanning through the tablet's live camera view until they saw me waving. The tablet's compass updated me on their orientation.

"This is Prof. Kumar, and Mr. Singh," said Krish, doing introductions.

"Nice to meet you, Daniel," said Prof. Kumar.

"Likewise, professor," I said.

"All right boys, you have our full attention," the Prof. said. "Explain…"

"So," Krish said, in true geek style… "Dan knows where we are, because my phone is logged in and registered into the virtual world we have created. We use a digital globe to fly to any location. We do that by using exact latitude and longitude coordinates." Krish looked at the Prof, who nodded. "So this way we can pick any location on Earth to meet at, provided of course, I'm physically present there."

"I understand," said the Prof. "Otherwise, it would be just a regular online multi-player game world."

"Precisely," Krish said. "What's unique here is a virtual person interacting with a real human in the real world. We're now on the campus Wifi." He circled his hand in front of his face as though pointing out to the invisible radio waves. "But it can also use a high-speed cell data network. The phone's GPS, gyro, and accelerometer updates as we move."

Krish explained the different sensor data to Mr. Singh and Professor Kumar. "We can use the phone as a sophisticated joystick to move our avatar in the virtual world that, for this demo, is a complete and accurate scale model of the real campus."

The Prof. was paying rapt attention to everything Krish had to say. "I laser scanned the playground and the food-court. The entire campus is a low rez 3D model," he said. "Dan can see us move around in the virtual world because my position updates. The front camera's video stream is also mapped to my avatar's face, so he can see my expressions."

"Now all we do is not render the virtual buildings, but instead, keep Daniel's avatar and replace it with the real-world view coming in through the phone's camera," explained Krish.

"Hmm... so you also do away with render overhead and possibly conserve battery life?" the Prof. asked.

"Correct. Using GPS, camera and marker-less tracking algorithms, we can update our position in the virtual world and sync Dan's avatar with our world."

"And we haven't even talked about how AI can enhance this," I said.

I walked a few steps away from them, counting as I went.

"We can either follow Dan or a few steps more and contact will be broken. This way in a social scenario, virtual people can interact with humans in the real world," Krish said. I was nearing the personal space out of range warning.

"Wait up, Dan," Krish called.

I stopped. He and the Prof. caught up.

"Here's how we establish contact," Krish said. He touched my avatar on the screen. I raised my hand in a high-five gesture.

"So only humans can initiate contact with these virtual people?" asked the Prof.

"Humans are always in control," I said.

"Aap Kaise ho?" Krish said.

"Main theek hoo," I answered a couple of seconds later, much to the surprise of the Prof. And finally to the interest of Mr. Singh, who leaned it to have a look.

"The AI module can analyze voice and cross-reference it with a bank of ten languages." he said. "Translation is done the moment it detects a pause in a sentence. This way multi-cultural communication is possible. I'm working on some features for the AI module. It will be based on computer vision libraries to study and recognize eyebrows and facial expressions. This data stream will then be accessible to the avatar's operator to carry out advanced interaction with people in the real world–"

"So people can have digital versions of themselves and do tasks in locations where they cannot be physically present," the Prof. completed Krish's sentence.

"Cannot or choose not to be present and in several locations if needed," I said. "There's no reason we can't own several digital versions of ourselves doing tasks simultaneously."

"Each one licensed with a unique digital fingerprint registered with the government or institutions offering digital surrogate facilities." Krish said.

"We call them di-rro-gates." I said. There was silence.

"Boys... this is big. We should consider looking into patents as well."

Krish looked into his phone camera. He was straining not to smile.

“Can this be tied to the FFT project?” Mr. Singh said, looking at the Prof.

“Err... FFT?” I asked.

“Friend and Foe Tracking. We abbreviate it to Double F-T. An upgrade project we're working on for the foreign militaries, Daniel. I could tell you more, if you're interested in coming here as a research guest.”

“Does this mean AYREE would fund our project?” said Krish. The Prof. looked at Mr. Singh. “If your ideas with this technology fit in with an existing AYREE project, we might,” he replied.

“We're perfecting a wearable version of this at AYREE Labs, as we speak. I'm sure you'll like it...” said Krish.

“Thank you boys. This is worth exploring, in-depth,” said the Prof. He and Mr. Singh left, leaving us crestfallen.

“I thought they'd jump at it,” I said.

“It's still half baked. We need to have a finished product to show. It's not going to work out this way...”

“You're right. Let's figure out a way to get this done. That's our priority,” I said. Krish pursed his lips and nodded in solemn agreement.

“The Prof. seemed genuinely interested. Let's do our best and have a little f–”

“–Faith? Faith, won't pay our bills. If we're gonna to do this, let's stick to logic only – OK?” I said. Krish stared at the scowl on my dirrogate's face.

...

I looked at the time on my phone: eight a.m–my midnight, and the phone was ringing. It was Kelly. A wave of guilt washed over me. I contemplated not answering.

"Hey, there. Still asleep?"

"No, no, up already." The hoarseness gave me away, but my voice sounded deep and Armstrong like.

"I got some news. Good news if you like."

"I could do with some of that. How's your trip going?"

"Nicely. I was talking to Daddy over breakfast this morning."

"Oh, OK, about?"

"Daddy's business is media and clubs, and I was thinking 'bout what you did the other night. I told him about the crowd going wild with the interaction onscreen, and he's very interested."

I kicked the covers off. She had my attention.

"What say we make this a feature at the club every weekend?"

"A job?" I asked.

"More than that. I was thinking from a commercial angle."

"For example?" I waited.

"Let's say it's a crowded Saturday night. You can't reach the bar. You could text the bar: "Send me the Saturday night special, balcony lounge"... or something like that. The Saturday night special would be sold to a brand who might be interested in paying for the promo."

"And this message flashes up on the big screen? Prestige

value for the punter?" I asked.

"Yeah that's an idea too. Customers would have to register their phones at the gate and buy credit, which gets deducted–"

"So we don't get assholes sending in messages," I said.

"Yup. Once the texted order is in, it gets acknowledged with a return code that the customer shows on his phone to the waiter when the drink arrives," she said.

"That's easy enough to do." That kind of coding was grade school programming. "So I get paid to implement such a brand entertainment system in the club?"

"Better than that. You can be my partner if you like, and we roll this out to other venues that Daddy owns."

I sat upright in bed. Passive income!

"Partners?" Kelly said.

"Why not," I said. "Any perks to this partnership?"

"You're an equal partner, not under me. So no perks," she teased.

"If it's all the same to you, I don't mind working under you from time to time."

"I'll have to remember to draft out a few sexual harassment clauses when I get back," she said.

"When are you back?"

"Saturday. Let's meet early in the day?" Her voice rose to make a more polite question of the statement.

"Sounds good. We can always continue after hours."

"Yeah, why not," she said.

It was an interesting turn of events. I liked working on

new ideas, and if it turned out to be a source of recurring income, it could be the break I was waiting for. A business where you got paid while having fun.

My idea engine was revving. I could take brand entertainment beyond nightclubs. Kelly said her dad was in the business of media as well. The AYREE project had potential, but Kelly's proposal was exciting. It meant clubbing, mixing with people, having a good time and getting paid. It meant more than getting paid, it was a business opp. I envied club owners but knew that it meant dealing with all sorts of questionable characters and that had its own set of problems. A business not for the fainthearted. Kelly's dad had to be powerful. Perhaps ruthless? I was getting involved with his daughter. I had to think everything through.

For the next few days I tried getting back to what Krish and I were working on but couldn't concentrate. I avoided two calls from him and Maya blaming my network. Without visual feedback, emotion was lost. Voice only conversations might as well be text. If the AR-driven project took off, it could propel his career. Was I being fair? Laser tunnels, the smell of fruity smoke, the throb of the bass beat and crowds at my command seduced me. Now there was Kelly. Guilt added to the seduction. I was giving in… drawn into a world where I was most comfortable.

Getting paid to live such a life had to be everyone's dream.

CHAPTER THREE

STATIC-SNOW ON MY PROJECTION screen still flashed from the disconnected call with Krish. In the lower right screen corner, a smaller PIP view of the A.I.R.I Campus 3D model slowly rotated. I was lounging on the couch, a can of beer in my hand enjoying the moment when the phone rang. I cleared my throat and answered the phone.

"Dan speaking... shoot."

The female voice on the other end said, "Sir, I've been

told to inform you, our Tower One project is on hold for now–"

"But... can you connect me to Mr.–"

"–Sir, he said he'll call you if there is a change."

I hung up before she said anymore and pounded my fist into the pillow on my couch repeatedly. I buried my face in the couch. It muffled my frustration.

...

Krish was in a Hospital room when he called me.

"Is the picture coming through?"

"Yeah, it's perfect. Is that a visor your dad is wearing?"

"Yes. A 3D printed prototype." I could see a faint smile on his father's face. "I thought it'd make him happy to visit in Virtual Reality, where his body can't take him, in real life," said Krish.

"Where's that?"

"A place, a sacred cave, some 12,000 feet above sea level - the Himalayas." Krish stepped away from the bed and came closer, his image almost filling my projection screen.

"He's always said his wish is to go on pilgrimage there before it's too late." He lowered his eyes. "I know we're going to lose him soon... It's best I come to terms with it." He walked back to his father to help him take off the visor.

"Ironically, this place he wants to visit, is where a Hindu God supposedly spelled out the secret to immortality."

"You're a good son, Krish. I'm sure he's proud of you."

"The visor's pretty crude right now, running AI routines using a smart-phone as server," said Krish.

"A Wi-zer!" I said. The term tripping out of my mouth. "With AI built in, it should be visor with a W."

"Brilliant," he said. "I was going for the unimaginative I-visor."

"So what's the A.I. do?"

"You'll have to come here and see for yourself. "I haven't shown it to the Prof. yet." He wore the visor. It looked like a pair of funky sunglasses.

"How'd you manage such a sleek profile?"

"It's all in the optics," he said. "Optical waveguide and other proprietary AYREE know-how bundled in."

"I gotta have that Wizer!" I said. I was an asshole not telling him that I was stalling. He could get an audience with the board members of AYREE with something like that. It could propel him up the ranks, yet he was treating everything as our project and waiting on me.

"I don't have cash right now for the trip–" It was a flimsy excuse, but I had to buy time to think this through and weigh it against Kelly's offer. "–and I'm sure getting a visa will take at least a week?" That was a better justification.

"Do you love her?"

"What? Don't start that crap again–"

"–I'm asking, because it's the A.I. running on the visor, or Wizer, as you call it... is reading your face and there's lots of red flags popping up."

"Meaning?" I asked.

"The A.I.'s reading your eyebrows, nostrils and pupil movement and referencing it to a database of techniques that interrogators use to read body language."

"You're analyzing me as we speak?"

"I thought a hands-on test was warranted," he said. "So getting back... is there something you're not telling me?"

"I need money. I'm three months overdue on everything. The scope deal is off too. I can't afford to come now."

"This is AYREE that's inviting and funding you. Visa, ticket, and stay is on them remember? "Once you're here, we can negotiate a daily pay for your working on this project, separate from selling ideas and royalties if the project has commercial potential."

"There's no guarantee of funding. That Mr. Singh, I'm not so sure about him. We're working on speculation, with these guys," I said.

"I told the Prof. the Wizer is your idea, your prototype, and that I'm using AYREE resources to refine it into a finished product for multiple markets," he said. "Both, the Prof. and Mr. Singh are keen to have you here." He took the Wizer off and looked straight into the camera.

"I need this, Dan. You know I do. It will solve both our problems, trust me." Krish looked at me, poker-faced. There was an uncomfortable moment of silence between us.

"Ummm... Let me sort things out here, alright?"

He nodded, disappointment showing on his face.

...

I had to sift through mounds of data from my heist at the Copa Cabbana, and I had been putting it off for a while. The door-bell rang. This time it was only the regular Pizza delivery guy, not my pizza goddess in purple underwear. I pulled out a can of beer from the refrigerator to wash down oversized bites as I went through slices of pepperoni spiced dough. The doorbell rang again.

"Go away, I've paid already," I groaned. The bell rang again. I walked up and flung it open. It was Lip-Gloss woman; Cheryl! She gave me the once over, and smiled, then lifted her hand twirling the 4-way adapter I'd lent them.

"Hi! How'd you find me?"

"Can I come in?" she said.

I stepped back, moving out of the way. She walked in, straight to the couch, and sat, crossing he legs, red toe-nails peeking from open pumps. I stood there watching her, still at a loss for words.

"Cozy place," she said. "I followed you the other day, Daniel. Just didn't have the nerve to come up, that time."

"How d'you know my name?"

Before she could say anything, I had another surprise. Blue blazer walked into the apartment. I was startled and nervous. I picked up a T-shirt from the floor and put it on.

"Oh, sorry, you remember MAGNUS, right?" she said. "We know a lot about you Daniel. Especially that primitive but ingenious trick - spoofing wifi access to skim data."

"Fuck. OK, I never steal people's credit info or anything, just corporate data. Are you Data Cops?" I asked.

Magnus and Cheryl laughed. Even her laugh was seductive.

"No, Daniel. We are you. Only, we do it the hard way; DNS poisoning." She uncrossed her legs and leaned forward. "We were tracking someone who's a regular at the Copa-Cabbana... until you show up with that cheap SSID spoofing, and our client connected to your access point."

"So, what is it you want? I'm not gonna go to that place anymore. You have my word." Fear showed in my voice.

"You have some data we need. It was not on your laptop. You make regular backups...ehh. Is good practice," said Magnus, his accent heavy, when he spoke. He smiled, more a smirk, then crossed his arms, muscles straining under his jacket.

"You're no hacker, Daniel. Just a resourceful guy. But when you spoof SSIDs with off-the shelf software, you keep your own back door... open."

"OK. Enough. We don't have time to play school," said Magnus. "Where is backups? I need to make copies. Now." Almost by reflex, I pointed to the portable drive near my laptop. Magnus walked over and opened his own laptop.

"Hey! there's personal data on that." I found my voice.

"Don't worry. We have no interest in your ah, home videos. Your laptop had some," said Cheryl. "She is cute, your girlfriend."

"You have no right to..."

"...to violate you, Daniel? You do the same, to others, right?" said Cheryl. She stood and walked over to peer over Magnus's shoulder. "Now, listen. We, Magnus and I, suggest you leave the country for a while. You might get into trouble here, if you don't."

"Leave the country? What?... Why?"

Magnus turned around, a shoulder holster showed through as his jacket opened.

"Consider it good, friendly advice. This, it goes deeper than you imagine," he said. He unplugged the drive from his laptop and stood, tucking his laptop under his arm.

"Of course, you're a sensible guy. Don't even think about telling anyone about our little – rendezvous," said Cheryl. She stepped closer and kissed me deliberately, on the cheek, leaving blood red lip prints. They left, closing the door behind them.

I was left with a choice. I optioned the easier one.

...

Business class was not a partition; it was a way of life, I soon learned. Living that life started the moment you walked to the check in counter. Plush red carpeting and velvet ropes set you apart from the herd. I would get a visit visa on arrival Krish had said, and AYREE had enough government connections to get a work permit when I was there. I settled in for the long flight ahead. It was already dark outside. I was a maharajah. It might have to do with the shape of the aircraft's windows. They reminded me of a palanquin from what I remember of period movies of India. It could have also been the piped Indian classical music drifting in and the textured cabin interiors.

I looked at the approaching flight attendant. She had her hair in a bun and wore a sari. Her bare midriff was sexy, but I couldn't help wondering what would happen if there was an emergency on the aircraft.

"Can I get you anything sir?"

"Uhh…white wine?" I said.

"With pleasure," she replied.

Relax, Dan. It's not a club, and she's seen better. I watched as two women entered the aircraft and made their way to seats a couple of rows in front of me. One of them looked like Maya. Maybe all pretty Indian girls looked alike. The other one glanced at me, doing a smooth double take. It had happened the first time Maya saw me at the club. I had Mom's skin tone and my dad's jawline and dark brown hair. I probably had his libido too. Dad had met Mom when she was on a study course in Rome and mistook her for an exotic mix of Italian and Mexican. She was charmed when he spoke a few lines from Bollywood movies, after she told him where she came from.

I took out my laptop. I had to get some ideas down on the use of the Wizer. Maya's smiling face with a wink was my wallpaper. In a few seconds, my overcrowded desktop icons obscured her face. I clicked a thumbnail on my desktop. It opened a photo taken a few weeks ago. She was looking through the scope. I should have carried the finished unit along to show Krish. The apartment was a mess when I'd left. I had remembered to shut the windows so dust would not get in. Maya had texted me to carry a few of her things... her naughty underwear and her favorite epilator from the bathroom. She also reminded me to get the glove. "In case we can't meet often," she had said. "Leave my toothbrush near the faucet and my lingerie in your closet."

"Why? It's not like you're coming back here."

"Yeah, but it will keep the bitches at bay."

Under that rebellious exterior, beat a real heart. I knew she was a rare find: intelligence, a palate for fine sex, yet she had her priorities right and morals intact. The text message indicated she was back to her cheerful self. She had come in second place at a classical dance recital, losing valuable points due to the limp. Nothing kept her down for long.

"Here you go, sir."

I took the wineglass by the stem, as the flight attendant set down a tray with the bottle.

"Thank you." I flashed her a smile.

Sipping wine, I began to think of uses for the Wizer. The first use that came to mind was as a friend-locater in a nightclub. The Wizer was already tinted, which made it look cool and killed the nerdiness factor associated with a pair of spectacles. I made a note to ask Krish if it was possible to use prescription lenses for people who needed glasses. Another concern was the sensitivity of the camera to the low lighting of a nightclub environment. There would be nothing worse than getting hit in the face by a woman because the AI in the Wizer misread her facial pattern! What also interested me was the idea of its possible use by the police and interrogators. One could analyze eyewitnesses or suspects without them knowing. Krish's AI combined with fuzzy logic processing in a wearable device such as the Wizer had far reaching uses. Augmenting information and visuals would mean having the required sensors embedded in the glasses or in a small wearable device. A wristwatch perhaps?

The wine was good. I poured the rest of the demi bottle into my glass, swirled and raised it to the light. The wine's legs were slow, long and supple. A man came walking down the aisle smiling. Did I know him?

I smiled back. He passed by my seat. He was only being polite. If I'd been wearing the Wizer, it could have matched his face with snapshots of known people and acquaintances and thrown up relevant info as he approached. I'd never have to be embarrassed again. Maybe there was a use for such a device for those dealing with memory loss? Augmenting information over the image of a loved one with a message: "This is your grandson," would help older people deal with failing memory. The only downside was if they misplaced their Wizer.

The wine was doing its thing. I didn't always get drunk at the club, but then again, wine was not my first choice in a nightclub. It had to be the air pressure at the altitude we were flying. I reached into the laptop bag and fished out my visor. Definitely not as sleek as the one Krish showed me, and the DIY job on the cameras was evident. But my visor had two OLED high resolution screens so movies could be enjoyed in 3D. I connected my phone and browsed my video library. I had a few stand-up shows and an old black and white 3D movie. Scrolling further through the list, a homemade clip of Maya came up, one of our couch sessions recorded in 3D.

I pressed play. There she was in full stereoscopic glory in my private movie theater, 35,000 feet high. Her toes pointing at me. I half smiled. Who needed movies in 3D? This was the reason people bought a 3DTV. Why didn't business class offer visors? Instead, they made it an embarrassing affair of having passengers dock their media players and browse personal videos on a screen embedded in a seat back. I adjusted the visor on my head, reclined my seat and settled in. The home video clip was only a few minutes. I switched to the old black and white movie.

"Ladies and Gentlemen." It was the pilot. "We are commencing our descent into Mumbai."

I took off the visor and squinted. The cabin lights had come on. There was a blanket draped over me up to my chest. I must have been a funny sight to the rest of the cabin crew, seeing me asleep with the visor on.

"Get you anything to freshen up, sir?"

"No, thanks. I'm good," I said.

...

Maya and Krish were there to meet me. We hugged each other. Maya's hug lingering longer. Krish looked the other way and helped with my luggage.

"I'm happy you've come. What made you change your

mind so fast?" he asked.

"Ahh... let's just say an angel paid me a visit and said I should go, like, now!"

Krish and Maya laughed. I put my arms around their waists, and we walked out of the terminal.

"I'm going to introduce you to Arjun. You sort of met his father - Mr. Singh; A powerful AYREE board member and financier."

I nodded, as we walked to the car park. A blast of muggy air hit us.

"It's a pleasure to drive through Mumbai at night," Krish said as we walked towards a brand new BMW X6. It stood out in contrast to the boxy cars and taxis around.

"Dan, this is Arjun. Arjun, Dan."

"Nice to meet you, Dan. I've heard a lot about you."

"Likewise, Arjun. Your name sounds familiar."

Arjun smiled. The X6 was negotiating potholes, splashing water sometimes, as puddles competed with tarred regions for street space. The road proved a challenge to German engineering. The local government could earn a good stream of revenue if manufacturers had their vehicles road tested in Mumbai. The city at night was a painting in contrasts. At eye level, the sulfur street lamps bathed its less fortunate inhabitants in a yellow cast. Pariah dogs running in small packs chased us out of the their turf as we slowed to avoid running over homeless people sleeping on sidewalks. Yet through the graduated tinted windows of the X6, the skyscrapers stood out, testament to the fact that there was a deep divide in the standard of living. A visible line of smog floated over the tops of the shanties, separating the lower city from the *beau monde.*

We slowed to take a filter lane, and the scenery changed. I sat up, the slight drowsiness disappearing at what I saw. Maya noticed. "That's Study Street."

I glued my face to the window and looked. Squatting in small circles under the cone of the overhead street light were young people with books in their laps. Some had lit bonfires and were sitting cross legged around it, their heads buried in the palms of their hands, reading.

"They live in cramped one room houses in the adjoining slums and colonies," Maya said. "It's too crowded at home for them to concentrate, so they come down here to Study Street."

We cruised past them, a few boys looking up from their books–rich man passing, they must have been thinking. Most did not bother looking at all. They were probably determined to better their lives.

"What happens when it rains?" I asked.

"They find a way. Resilience and ingenuity is what helps them survive," Krish said. Arjun waved his hand in a dismissing gesture.

A sharp turn later, we were at the imposing gates of AIRI. Spotlights accentuated the chrome words: "Artificial Intelligence Research Incubator." They were set in relief on a granite plaque sticking out of the ground. The guard left the guard-box, shielding his eyes from the glare of the headlights, and approached Arjun's side of the car. He rolled down the window, and stood at attention with a salute. He hastened to his cubicle, and the iron gates rolled back.

We were on the path leading through the manicured lawns of the campus. It was a strange feeling of déjà vu. I knew we would next make the hairpin bend to arrive at the three story–visiting faculty and guest residence–building.

"I'm sure you'll like your apartment," Arjun said. "It has an attached terrace."

Maya looked at me and mouthed a silent "Ooohh," her eyes sparkling and her eyebrows doing a mischievous dance. I had tried imitating that whenever I had a mirror in front of me but could never quite gain control of only one eyebrow at a time.

"Cool. Thanks, Arjun."

"Our pleasure," he said. "If you need anything, you just ask. We'll give you the royal treatment here. After all, you've come highly recommended."

"Ahh, most work's being done by your resident genius Krish. I'm his wingman."

He shifted his gaze from Krish to me, then realized Maya was looking. "Right-right, good," he said.

The apartment was better than I imagined. It was luxury. White sheer curtains adorned the windows, and the drapes were secured to the sides with elegant rope ties. A bit feminine for my taste, but it looked rich. It was a one bedroom apartment though quite spacious, and the living room had floor-to-ceiling glass that slid open to allow access to the terrace. The terrace itself ran the length of the living room and bedroom.

"I got them to set up a deck chair," Arjun said, pointing to the sun lounger that kind of looked out-of-place with no pool. Maya went back into the living room and emerged with two cushions and a throw. She knelt on the lounger arranging the cushions. Arjun ran to her side and held her hand, taking the cushions from her and helping her up.

"No, no, Maya, allow me. We will make sure that our guest is comfortable during his stay here. I'll have facilities management assign someone 24/7 to look into it."

"That's OK. I'm sure I'll be fine. I don't need 24/7 help," I said. I treasured my privacy over anything else.

"Nonsense. Your comfort is our priority. Your man Friday will be right next door in his quarters. You just need to ring."

"Well, then! That works for me. Thanks."

So that's how organizations seduced employees into selling their souls! We went back into the living room. Arjun's phone rang. He opened the glass door to the terrace and shut it behind him. Krish had to use the bathroom, leaving Maya and me alone for the first time.

We seized the moment. Our lips met, and her tongue sought mine. I could feel a charge shoot from deep in my chest and radiate over as my brain finally registered and then locked onto that familiar sensation. She grabbed the back of my head. It was a stolen kiss. Past her shoulder I could see Arjun's shadowy profile. He was leaning over the far side rail, one hand pressing the phone to his ear the other hand scratching and twirling his hair.

"Missed you, baby. Missed you a lot."

"You've never said it in that voice before," she said.

"What voice? It must be the change in weather here."

"It's OK to show how you feel once in a while you know," she said, her eyes seeking mine. I kissed the tip of her nose. We heard the toilet flush. Krish walked out of the bath-room and saw us sitting at opposite ends of the small dining table. I flicked through channels on the TV with the remote. Late-night Bollywood music videos were playing. Close-ups of cleavage encased in colorful costumes rhythmically thrust at the camera. It got a bit embarrassing.

"Welcome to Bollywood!" Arjun said, closing the door behind him. We forced a laugh. "It's late. I'm sure our guest needs to rest. Let's meet for brunch tomorrow if it's OK? We can take you on a tour of the campus and meet the others. Will you be joining us Maya?" asked Arjun.

"Oh, no. I'm spending the day with Mama. Maybe later in the evening."

"Do you guys live far from here?" I asked.

"Not that far. I think you could see Krish's building from your terrace with a pair of binoculars," Arjun said.

"Cool. Brunch it is then," I said.

"I'm sure the Prof. is keen to meet you in person," Krish said.

I showed them to the door, shaking hands with Arjun first, then Krish and lingering a bit longer with Maya.

"Oh, wait. Here's the things you asked for." I handed Maya a bag.

"Thanks a ton," she said, ears turning a shade of red.

I closed the door and turned the AC control a few notches down. It wasn't hot in Mumbai at night, but twenty degrees had a special meaning to me. It spelled a-good-life. I was exhausted though I'd fallen asleep on the aircraft. I lay in bed watching the sheer curtains float as they caught the draft from the vents. I tried to sleep, but my thoughts kept jumping around between how to go about making a good first impression on the Prof. and what part of the project to concentrate on to generate tangible results faster.

In reality, Arjun and Maya monopolized my thoughts. Was I getting possessive? envious? jealous? The guy had everything. He reeked of money, had a good car; it was a fucking good car, compared to the majority of boxy vehicles that I'd seen on the drive from the airport. It might not even be the only one he owned. I could bet he didn't need to worry about getting into a DJ cabin or the VIP room at a club. He might just be the owner of one. In retrospect, the bastard was not bad looking either. The only thing he didn't have was Maya!

She was not an accessory. She couldn't be owned and she was not a perk either. Silicon-filled bimbos were perks. Maya was more… without the need for artificial enhancements. Her body was fab; I couldn't argue with that. But she always said it was a by-product of discipline. "Anything and everything in moderation," was her motto. To me, her best assets were her morals. I'd been on the circuit long enough to know the difference. It was near impossible to find that quality in a woman.

Back home I was king, and a club was my kingdom. None of my subjects ever complained. Beef cakes were never any challenge, they were always a turnoff the moment they opened their mouths to speak. Unless a woman was after a dumb fuck. But that was my turf. This...was Arjun's. He didn't come across as an ass. What if Maya gave in? She wasn't repulsed by him. Was she giving me something to think about? She wanted us to be much more than fuck buddies with an after-play protocol, and I always managed to steer clear of any kind of commitment. Arjun would have her mom's blessing. Krish might even get a stake in the organization. Everyone would win.

Except me.

I tried to swap out the thought by going through other threads in my mind. Sleep came, like the smog down at Study Street… engulfing me.

…

I woke to the faint cawing of crows. My cell-phone display read 11:00 a.m. I had slept well and couldn't remember any specific dream, although I realized I did have dreams the previous night. I went into the bathroom and ran the faucet. The water tasted different, almost sweet. Non desalinated water tasted that way I figured.

There were two knocks on the main door.

"Good morning, sir." It was a male voice.

I grabbed an over-sized towel, wrapped it around my waist and walked to the door.

"Are you awake, sir?" The question was followed by another knock.

I opened the door and found myself looking down at a smiling face. He was about five-five and looked to be about 40 to 45 years, with an unshaven graying but groomed beard and mustache.

"My name is Ram Bhai." He joined his hands in a "Namaste" greeting. "If there is anything you need in your stay, I do my best."

"Hi, Ram bhai. Thank you. I'm Dan."

"Please to meet you, Sir Dan."

That sounded funky. I wondered how it would sound on a party flyer: "Featuring: Sir Dan." Ram bhai interrupted my imperial self-reflection. "Arjun and Krish sir, are waiting for you at faculty lounge. I take you there when ready."

"Right. I'll need about 15 minutes."

"No problem. I wait next door."

I had a quick shower, wincing as the lukewarm water ran over me. There hadn't been enough time for the overhead heater to raise the temperature. I would be meeting the Prof. face to face. I considered wearing a tie and jacket but settled for a pair of jeans, a t-shirt and brown corduroy blazer. It showed respect yet didn't look stiff. Ram bhai was standing outside my door.

"Follow me. I take you there."

I let him lead, although I was confident of making my way around the campus. I had a detailed model of the campus on my phone from the virtual meetings with Krish. The mix of people at the main building was intriguing. I hadn't expected so many blond-haired people. With most of the first world under recession, India beckoned no doubt. The building itself could put most institutions I'd seen in so called developed countries to shame. The glint of what looked like gold specks embedded in the black floor tiles caught my eye as I part walked, part strutted down the foyer. The glass and marble interiors of the building announced world class infrastructure. A mix of semi casual and business suited people created a serious yet trendy atmosphere. We took the elevator to the first floor and turned right to face a door with a plaque that read: Faculty Lounge. Ram bhai smiled, joined his hands, and did a little bow.

"I go back and wait at guesthouse building."

I thanked him and pushed the door open.

"Dan!" I heard Krish, and turned around to locate him. He waved me over to a long corner table with him and Arjun.

So he had come after all, protecting Daddy's investments. I had to act mature and keep personal envy and bias out. He hadn't done anything or said anything wrong since I arrived. If anything, Arjun had been only nice to me.

"Sleep well, Dan?" Arjun asked.

"Like I was stoned."

"Good, good. We can arrange for that if you like later tonight." He smiled. "Krish tells me you're a DJ as well?"

"He has a following back home when he plays," Krish said.

"We should do it then. Let's go to our club this Saturday."

Our club... I knew it!

Krish and Arjun stood at attention.

"Sit, sit, boys." I recognized the voice: Professor Kumar. I turned and stood, extending my hand.

"Good to see you in real life, Daniel. You lost body mass since we last met." We laughed.

"The six-pack abs and biceps are the fantasy version of myself." I shook his hand. "It's an honor to be here Professor Kumar."

"Our pleasure, Daniel. Krish and you show some incredible potential." The Prof. gestured for us to sit. "You've met Arjun I see. His father is one of the main supporters of AYREE, and it's thanks to his blessings that we have the kind of budgets for R&D that make us the envy of other IT incubators and research facilities. Arjun has shown great interest in our work, and after I presented your project to the board, his father pledged funds and gave us a blanket go-ahead to work on a prototype."

"Dad and I believe in breaking ground, while others only follow," Arjun jumped in.

"Arjun will shadow both of you on the project. Part of the reason is for accounting purposes to satisfy the board–"

"But the bigger reason is that I see we will be creating something of unique value," Arjun said.

I wasn't sure whether his interjection was genuine enthusiasm or him wanting to affirm ownership. I had to stop projecting negativity, or there would be no progress.

"I won't be in your faces all the time, guys. I'd like it if you invite me to any big breakthroughs though! After the Prof. explained to us an outline of what Krish and you, Dan, are working on, I'm too fascinated to not want to be part of this. I just wish I could be an active contributor."

"You're funding it. Without that contribution there is no project," I said. Never bite the hand that... Mom's adage came to mind.

"The board is funding it, and Professor Kumar believes in it," he said, his voice low. "Let's do our best. A lot of AYREE's resources are being rerouted to this project."

CHAPTER FOUR

"I'M DOWNSTAIRS," KRISH SAID on the phone. "We've got about 30 minutes before Mr. Singh arrives."

I had been in Mumbai for a week, and the combination of Indian food and the sultry weather was working its magic on me. I'd overslept, knowing full well it was an important day for all of us.

"I'm carrying the Mesh Arm Cast. It's powered and ready to go," he said.

"Great. So everything's working fine?"

"Yes, it should be. Why don't you come to the grounds. It'll save time."

"Sure. I'll see you there in about fifteen minutes."

Krish and AYREE engineering had worked overtime and 3D printed more Wizers. The new build had substantial modifications. It had two embedded cameras with a wider field of view. I glanced at it lying by my bedside. It weighed no more than a pair of chunky sports sunglasses, with bone conduction audio technology. I was down fifteen minutes later, and slipping prototype AYREE technology on my right arm. First came the futuristic Three Finger Glove – Black, with chrome knuckles; a carbon fiber composite exoskeleton, encasing my thumb, index and middle finger. I flexed my fingers and the glove calibrated with two high pitched whizzing sounds. Next, it was time to slip my right arm into the Mesh Arm Cast. I slipped off my T-shirt and Krish held it while I placed my arm in the cast. The alloy clasps adjusted to my arm for a snug fit. This was every guy's super-hero fantasy come true.

Krish ran back to his laptop. Some last minute tweaks to the Wizer or his code, I suspected. I wore my Wizer and adjusted the slider until the cross polarizers attenuated the bright daylight a few shades. The Wizer became an expensive pair of sunglasses.

"Building game world," I said to Krish, echoing the message on the display as it connected to the campus network.

"Uh huh, same here."

I heard him clearly. The Wizers arms pressed against my

temples transferring his raspy voice. The cameras embedded at the outer edges of the Wizer started and were triangulating and constructing a synthetic version of the real environment from the 3D video streams coming in.

The engineering team at AYREE had done a slick job embedding those tiny cameras. Using the same code tweaked from the tests we'd done for the Prof. and Mr. Singh, the Wizer was given the ability to generate a depth map of everything in its field of view. I moved my head from side to side in an arc. A 3D model of the real world was taking shape in real-time. The video was draped over. Synthetic Krish looked awesome and was moving in perfect registration over real Krish.

"Could I replace you with a brunette instead? I asked.

"Using blob tracking and feature recognition I think we could assign a human mesh at the same position I am and have my actions drive its IK skelet–"

"–Woah there! I was only speaking in jest," I said. He always took every question seriously. A few moments later, the Wizer synced to the Mesh Arm Cast, and displayed a list of options. He had updated the interface. "Choose Cricket," he said.

I lifted my gloved hand. The Wizer's cameras triangulated my finger in 3D space and knew where I was pointing. In an instant, 3D imagery filled my field of view and a Cricket pitch that looked like a short runway with wooden stumps on either side locked on and got overlaid between us. I hit the info button, and the virtual Cricket pitch had text over it, telling me that the stumps were indeed called stumps in the game. There were three of them on both ends of the pitch and two smaller pieces of wood, called bales, balanced on the stumps. Krish had a real bat and ball in his hands. He threw the ball to me. As he moved, he occluded the virtual stumps, as if they were actual wooden spikes in the ground. I adjusted the transparency slider on the Wizer and removed the layer of video draped depth mapped geometry, leaving the game layer of pitch and stumps perfectly aligned to the real ground.

"Watch this," he said. Virtual shrubbery came up near the pitch, flanked with a few clumps of tall grass, gently swaying.

"Amazing! I like the added touch of the animated grass."

"Thanks to our environment artist, Satish. By the way, in case you didn't notice, the grass blades are catching the wind in the same direction as the real tree." He pointed to a palm tree nearby.

"How? Internet weather update?" I asked.

"We could do it that way as well. But we have weather sensors on the main campus building. The Wizer is tapping into the central server for an accurate reading. The server's doing all the heavy lifting and feeding the animated imagery back."

I stopped for a moment to admire the work of the environment artist and wondered if there'd be enough compute power some day to embed such realistic rendering within the Wizer itself. AYREE was working on it, Krish had said.

"Give it a few minutes. The AI module is building a framework of the environment and a profile of you," he said.

"Profile of me - or for me?"

"Of. We'll add to your profile later. The AI can learn your daily routine your preferences, your habits - so to speak."

"What for? Isn't that overkill?" I asked. "Do I have to program all this?"

"I didn't have time to dumb down the AI routines. You've got the entire library with you. Everything that the algorithms can currently do - from computer vision routines - to environment learning modules, is all in there." He tapped the bat to the ground. I could hear it loud and clear across the pitch.

"Think of it as recording your preferences and style," he said. "This data is stored in a database. The learning module is now sampling this current location and time of day. It's collecting data of what the wearer does, as well as point clouds of the environment. I'm looking at what to do with all the data."

"OK, but what do you mean recording my preferences?"

"It's building what's called a frame of the activity we are doing now. Let's call it the game frame. Later I'll show you how to create and populate your apartment frame."

"Huh? You're losing me with the digitalk."

"It's quite simple, you'll get it soon enough," he said. "For instance, in an Apartment Frame, over the course of a week– say eight a.m. every day–the AI triggers the camera sensor on the Wizer." Krish swung the bat in the air as though aiming to hit an imaginary ball out to the campus perimeter. I heard him take a deep breath. "It compares the snapshot to previous snapshots and data gathered at eight. If it sees only images of your morning bedroom, then it's logical for the AI to deduce it's either the weekend or you've overslept."

"I don't see any usefulness in that piece of intelligence."

"Yes, I don't either right now. If the algorithm performs well enough, maybe we could find some simple uses for it by tying a few if-then constructs."

"Meaning?"

He looked at the Wizer's display. The frame was still being built. "Say it's not the weekend, so when the A.I. interrogates the camera for a snapshot of the environment in the morning, the AI could then ring an alarm or connect to your home automation hub and run your a.m. routine of starting your espresso machine and water heater."

"Cool, so the AI could automate my morning chores," I said. "It would know that I like a cup of coffee and a shower before I leave?"

"Yes. By analyzing snapshots at different times of day, it creates these frames or containers of the different locations you frequent and the typical actions you perform.

"So I don't need to create these frames myself?"

"I'm experimenting. The two cameras on the Wizer help the AI learn by digitizing locations in full 3D, segmenting and isolating distinct objects and then comparing them to its existing bank of entities, locations and actions."

"So while I walk around wearing the Wizer, in the background the AI is visually sampling the environment and comparing what it sees with its memory bank?"

"You're catching on fast," he said. "Yes, it's running routines that are the outcome of ongoing advances in computer vision know-how using stereoscopic image processing libraries.

"My code takes forward classic AI logic from the 'seventies, and I'm hoping my algorithm can now make judgment calls on creating its own master frames at a macro level, based on entities and subjects that it sees in different locations."

As Krish spoke about AI and the algorithm he was working on, the far reaching implications and possibilities of a world with augmented intelligence became clearer. After all, if there was a depth map of the real world, inserting smart digital content into it would be progress in the right direction.

"Humans are creatures of habit," he said. "We live our lives following the same routine day after day. We do the things we do with one primary motivation–comfort."

"That's not entirely true," I said. "What about random acts. Haven't you done something crazy or on impulse?"

"Even randomness is within a set of parameters; thresholds," he said.

"Unless you're eccentric," I said.

"The aim of our research in Artificial Intelligence is not to cater to eccentricity. My AI algorithm is a child… learning by observing and referencing."

"So no impulse subroutines in your code then?"

"Impulse is a human anomaly. Works at times but also a cause for regret many a time."

"So, what you're saying is A.I. does not need to ape human intelligence."

"I would prefer it didn't. But to make it more acceptable, my code does have some randomness thrown in."

"Within parameters, I suppose?"

"Yes, the random subroutine will only execute within safe parameters when straying from the norm."

The Wizer had completed its initiation routine and came to life as I got it out of power saving mode. It overlaid a dotted red line to one of the stumps peeking through between the bat and Krish. He was knocking the bat to the ground, a slow and steady tap tap tap. As he moved, the line fluctuated its trajectory to where I was supposed to aim and lob the ball.

"All right. Let's do this," he said.

Though we were a good hundred yards apart, I heard him as though he stood right besides me. I held out my hand and a virtual replica overlaid itself over mine, curling its thumb, index finger and ring finger over a computer generated ball, its seam glowing red. The animation played repeatedly. The Three Finger Glove whirred – my fingers spinning the ball. The virtual ball still had a red seam. Within seconds, the real ball's seam lined up with the simulated one.

Green. I was good to go!

The red line then dipped in front of his bat and rose again to lock onto the stump still showing between his leg and bat. I was going to be bowling a curved ball. Using the red line as a guide, I aimed at the stumps, lifted my leg baseball pitcher style, and before he could protest, I let the ball fly. He stood rooted to the spot. The virtual stumps, bales and all, spun out as if hit by a missile. "Goal!" I punched the air and did a victory shuffle.

"This is not soccer!"

I winced and pulled the Wizer off.

"Sorry, didn't mean to yell, but you have a little more to learn about cricket, and it's beyond the scope of the AI at this moment," Krish said.

"Whatever! I nailed your ass!"

"Only because I let you," he said.

I forgot we had two Wizers. Defense or counterattack was always an option. We were interrupted by the loud WHOP-WHOP-WHOP-WHOP of a helicopter's blades, coming in for a landing. Krish and I watched as it touched down some 50 yards away. The doors opened and Mr. Singh, Arjun and the Prof. alighted and made their way toward us. We folded our Wizers and walked up to them.

"Gentlemen, I have only a little time then, I'm afraid," said Mr. Singh, over the sound of the rotors. "I hope there's more than cricket to see?" He gestured to the bat Krish was holding. Krish looked nervous.

"Yes there is. Let me introduce you to the Wizer," I said, lowering my voice mid sentence as the chopper's rotors slowly came to a halt. "We call it Wizer, with a 'W', because it augments human intelligence."

Mr. Singh looked up, raising an eyebrow. "A demo for me? Now?"

"Sure."

As they looked on, I extended my right hand and rolled up my shirt sleeve, up to my elbow. My arm right down to my wrist was encased in the carbon fiber Mesh Arm Cast. Sliding the collar of my T-shirt exposed the shoulder part of the cast with a recessed button. Pressing down on the button brought my exoskeleton encased arm to life with a short electronic whine.

"We've borrowed this prototype exoskeleton from a physiatry project that AYREE engineering is working on for the Indian Army."

Mr. Singh and Arjun looked at each other. The Prof. looked at Krish. I rolled my shoulder and flexed my arm a few times. There was complete silence when I spoke next, except for the chirping of birds in the field.

"I could tell you about an Augmented Cricket module, but that would'nt do justice to what we are about to show you." I flexed my fingers, the electro mechanical feedback sounded both re-assuring and hi-tech. "You see, traditional Double F-T is for showing the location of friendly military forces and enemies...Yes, I had to look that up."

I walked to my backpack on the grass, and fished out my laptop showing a them the screen with a terrain mesh overlaid over the field we were in, and with scattered dots in blue and red. Krish distributed Wizers to the three of them.

"One of the easier things to do with the Wizer, is to allow soldiers to visualize these individual blips as Digital Surrogates, augmented within their field of view." I said, tapping the arm of my Wizer twice.

Holographic like CG soldiers were superimposed over the ground; spread out. Some in blue, and some in scattered clusters of red.

"But, with Krish's AI algorithms, we can do so much more. See that dustbin at the far end of the field?"

Mr. Singh slipped the Wizer over his eyes. The Prof. and Arjun mimicked him. Through our Wizers, all of us saw a yellow gun-sight like target hovering over a red soldier who was in turn, attached to the dustbin. The view automatically zoomed to a closeup of the dustbin with the sniper cross-hairs superimposed. I picked up another cricket ball and gestured with my hand in front of my Wizer, selecting the FFT module. In a matter of seconds, my right arm went stiff and moved of it's own accord, arcing almost 180 degrees behind me...

Woooosh!! My hand pitched the ball, using my shoulder as the pivot. The Ball-missile flew through the air and connected with the metal dustbin at the far end of the field with a distant, THWOP! The dustbin went flying off it's holder. The view zoomed to show the dustbin severely dented with the yellow target overlay still tracking it, the red Digital Surrogate soldier lay prone on the ground. Mr. Singh, Arjun and the Prof. watch in stunned silence.

Mr. Singh then brought his hands together and clapped. The

others took their cue from him. Krish was beaming, while I smiled and nursed my arm from the aftershock. After we'd had our moment, I got back to the demo...

“Soldiers can run preset AI libraries, on-demand. A Cricket sim allows a soldier stationed in a foreign land to interact and win the confidence of locals.” Now Mr. Singh was a student, paying rapt attention. “Think, foreign commando in Pakistan becoming a cricket or soccer expert - you get the idea,” I said.

“Impressive,” said Mr. Singh. “I had a feeling you were an investment worth pursuing. Didn't I say, Arjun?” Arjun nodded and patted Krish on the back. He came and shook my hand. “Well done!” he said. But I was'nt yet done. We, Krish and I, were'nt done. We had to impress them, a lot of our future was riding on the demo.

“Krish's AI libraries are actually, living code; constantly evolving. The AI is always updating itself, getting sensory input via the Wizer. Am I right Krish?”
Krish nodded in the affirmative.

“A soldier can augment his or her intelligence, the more they wear the Wizer. The data stream can also be accessed by a remote observer - a coach, if you will.” I looked around.

“Let's improvise, shall we?” I beckoned them to follow. We walked toward the helicopter. Mr. Singh waved to the pilot to allow me access to the cockpit. I put the Wizer back on and the cockpit was transformed to a live grayscale depth image. Yellow circles and twisty lines contorted, tracked and locked onto the dial gauges and switches on the dashboard.

As the Wizer recognized the shape of controls, graphical outlines conformed to the physical contours and turned green. Color then returned to my view.

"The Wizer's identified this bird as an IAL 300. Is that right, sir?" I turned to the Pilot, seeing him through the Wizer. The Pilot nodded - Yes. My view got superimposed with options. I selected the Exec icon, with a stab of my finger in midair. A sequence of numbers got overlaid over the switches and controls in the cockpit. My glove encased index finger, as if on autopilot, began to flip them ON, one by one - The rotors started. I saw panic on the Pilot's face.

"I won't. I'm not licensed...yet," I said. I smiled and it calmed him. He sat back in his seat.

""You know, in movies when they get operations manuals downloaded to their brains? Well that's just Sci-fi masturbation," I said. "This, now this, is real."

The pilot looked on nervously, tracking my hand with his gaze, as I positioned it over the shaft, my thumb, driven by the glove, automatically curling over the top.

"Sir, what happens if I pull back on this?"

"We will have lift-off," he said.

I tapped the Wizer, and my index finger began to disengage the controls.

"And that... gentlemen, is how we upgrade the military."

As the rotors started to wind down, I exited the cockpit and bowed with an exaggerated flourish. Everyone exited the chopper with a round of applause.

"I am late, but a delay like this was certainly worth it!"

He turned to the Prof. "Krish is working on DRONE?"

"Very much indeed," said the Prof.

"What's drone?" I asked.

"It's classified, Dan. I couldn't tell you," Krish said.

"I want Daniel on DRONE too," said Mr. Singh.

"We can't get clearance for him this late and besides he's a foreigner. He would need additional background checks," Arjun said.

"I want part of the lab at AYREE secured off and connected to DRONE," said Mr. Singh. "We will make DRONE part of the project work that Daniel is working on and make sure he is suitably compensated. I leave those discussions between you and the professor, Daniel," he said.

"Sounds exciting," was all I could say.

"How do we coordinate between locations?" Arjun asked.

"Digital surrogate?" I blurted. Krish's face lit up.

"This weekend, we celebrate," said Mr. Singh. "Arjun will send a car for you."

...

Krish and I walked to the AYREE parking lot feeling elated. We talked about more uses for Wizer technology. The military usage of technology was something that Krish had reservations about, and to a certain extent, so did I. There was no denying that funding for work, sadly, only came via military projects.

"We already have a proof of concept of the interrogation module for the police and investigations departments. A great use of AI and AR," he said. "Now how about in physio therapy? A module that shows limb movement overlaid like the pro cricket player gripping the ball correctly. The idea is to get AYREE's board to invest in manufacturing the Wizer and bringing the price down to affordable levels."

"A first aid module?" I asked.

"For paramedics," he said. "A Wizer in every home can possibly save people's lives. How many know CPR today?"

He stopped walking and turned to look at me.

"So, let's imagine a module overlaying a human avatar over a body on the floor," I said. "Simple gestures or the feature tracking itself can scale the avatar to match the size of the body, adult or child, and then a CPR procedure is played out for the aid giver to follow."

He nodded. "When an emergency occurs, most people panic. The AI could activate in the background and make a decision on calling emergency services after a given amount of time has elapsed... these are tweaks we could build in." I could tell he was beginning to like the idea.

"Hmm..." he said. "After all, the AI is constantly taking snapshots of the environment, segmenting and cross-referencing the home frame." Krish was doing that thing he did when his brain was about to get hit by a million hypnotic Theta and Gamma waves at the same time–He put both hands to his head and drummed his fingers on his scalp, his gaze fixed to a shrub on the ground which I thought would incinerate under the intensity of his stare.

Eventually he spoke again: "So, maybe the AI accesses the current frame, references time of day, and using a gestalt subroutine, figures something is not right with a person in a slumped position. The skeletal overlay could do that–"

I interrupted him. "Uh huh. Yeah, I'll leave the jargon to you. In essence what I mean is if the AI sees a person lying askew on the floor it can figure something's not right by accessing feedback from the cameras. Facial expressions can easily be isolated from a stereo pair and perhaps pulse irregularity can be gleaned from image brightness, right?"

"Pulse reading from image brightness would depend on the fidelity of the image, but facial expressions, yes," he said. "And if someone's collapsed on the floor, chances are there will be a skeletal mismatch with the superimposed human IK rig."

"So… let's build a complete frame of my apartment, run a few tests and invite the Prof. over," I said.

"You want to act out an emergency heart attack scenario?" Krish asked.

"That's right. Both of you can have Wizers on and witness it firsthand."

"What happens if a person lives alone?" he asked.

"In that case, we port the AI to a wall mounted FishEye."

"Lesser cost than a wearable Wizer. I like the idea!" he said. "People in panic need augmented intelligence."

"You're almost there. Look who's spouting bylines now!" We reached the parking lot, and he straightened his bike and kicked the stand back in place. He had a nice motorcycle, reminding me of a Harley fat boy, but his was a Royal Enfield. I hadn't seen one before. Krish told me he had customized it. The original wheels were too skinny. I supposed a bike was better suited to the congestion in the city. He kick started it and I nodded in approval. The motor sounded sexy. It had a deep throbbing rumble. James would have loved to sample that as an LFE track for the groove rider.

"Freshen up, and we chat later?" Krish said.

"Yeah, I guess so. We need to be on a war footing with this. See you tomorrow at the lab?"

"I'll be at Drone HQ. We'll link up via Dirrogates." He revved the 500cc engine and took off. I made my way back to the guest building. I was looking forward to the club, not so much for the entertainment but for the chance to impress on Arjun's father that his investment in us would pay dividends he never expected.

...

I reached the apartment and found the door ajar. I let the pilo erection at the back of my neck subside in an attempt to channel the adrenaline surge. I lifted the cricket bat I was carrying and poked at the door till it opened wide. The lamp at the far end of the room was the only light, and the white curtains were flapping in the wind. Had I been robbed?

I took a few steps back and on instinct took my cell phone out. The wise thing would be to call Krish. Did 911 work? Was 911 the international code for emergencies? I was about to dial him, when my phone rang. I jumped, and the phone almost slipped out of my hand. It was Kelly. I cut the call as my peripheral vision glimpsed a shadowy figure move behind the curtain and enter the living room

"Who's there?" I called, cricket bat at ready.

"Sir–you are back." It was Ram bhai.

"How did you get in here?"

"Sorry, sir. Arjun sir asked me to put new lounge chair on terrace."

"I didn't know you had a key," I said, somewhat relieved that it was Ram bhai.

"I don't, sir. Security opened for me to put the chair. He is sitting in my room." The security guard must have heard my voice and was standing outside.

"Oh, OK." I calmed down. "I thought I had been robbed."

"Sorry, sir. I keep door open, maybe wind from the terrace closed it." Ram bhai bowed and left with the security guard. I shut the door behind them and switched on the lights. The terrace door was still open. I stepped out to admire the expensive and futuristic looking white chaise longue. There was also a bar counter on wheels stocked with bottles and glasses. On top of it was a boombox with a CD wrapped in a ribbon. I looked at the cover: Selected Chill-out Classics. Arjun was generous. I could get used to such a life. I stretched out on the lounger, sinking into the richness of the memory foam cushion. The phone beeped.

It was a message from Kelly.

"Sorry I guess you're busy with some whore huh? Call me when free."

The bar had one of my favorites: Malibu. The white bottle with its distinct coconut flavored rum was irresistible. I had to go inside for ice. Kelly's number was busy. I tried it again.

"Wish you had called a few minutes ago," she said.

"Why?"

"You would have heard me whimpering."

She reminded me so much of Maya it was spooky. Kelly was everything a guy could want in a fuck buddy. I pushed my luck. "Can you go again?"

"For you… hmmm."

I was walking a fine line.

"Uhh, maybe a rain check," I said.

"I knew it. Who is she? Is she good?"

"There's no one, but who knows. Maybe this weekend I meet someone. Invited to a club."

"You're making me jealous, Dan. I should come there, if you won't come here. We also have work to discuss, remember?"

"I've not forgotten. Looking at wrapping things here, and I'll be back."

"OK. Talk soon." She cut the call abruptly.

I looked at the phone, puzzled. My mouth was still open from an unfinished bye-bye. Delayed gratification always led to handsome rewards. It was getting late. I jumped in for a quick shower. Krish and I needed to collaborate with the others in the lab to get some ideas finished. I made a mental note to speak to him about setting time aside to meet on a regular basis with other programmers there. We needed structure and a project timeline if we were to come up with finished modules.

...

The Phone rang. It was 8 a.m. My head was pounding, from the mix of whatever I'd concocted at my terrace bar.

"Dan, I need you in the lab ASAP. The Prof. and Mr. Singh are on their way here."

It was unlike Krish to dispense with pleasantries. It had to be urgent.

"Gimme about 15 minutes. What's project drone anyway?"

"I'll tell you once you're in the lab. Now get moving."

Splashing water on my face didn't get rid of the smell of stale nightclub air on me, so I jumped into the shower. Exactly 15 minutes later I was at the AYREE campus and in Krish's section of the lab. It was cordoned off and had two men inside whom I did not recognize as regular staff.

"Good morning, Mr. Daniel," said one of them. "We are from DRONE and will be stationed as observers. Feel free to continue your work. We won't be in the way."

"Good morning to you as well," I said. I didn't like the idea of people peering over my shoulders, but I was curious to know what drone was. I was promised extra compensation in exchange for my knowledge. That was incentive enough. I called Krish.

"I'm at the lab. Am I visiting you, or are you tele-travelling here?"

"You're visiting," he said. "I've set up the room. Launch the app and we're good to go"

I flicked through the apps menu on my phone and waited for the overhead camera to link via wifi.

"I need coordinates," I said.

"N 39° 1'12.2664, E 1° 28'55.7646." He read them out. I waited while the lab's high-speed network made the connection. A few moments later, my Wizer immersed me in a white, sterile looking room, the kind from sci-fi movies. Krish and the Prof. were there dressed in yellow overalls, and both had Wizers on. The whole scene looked surreal. The Prof, Krish and a section of the white room were located on a beach. Krish had used a stock video background of a stretch of beach with aqua blue water gently lapping the shore. The ambient sound of the surf was a nice touch. I turned my head and saw landmarks of a familiar beachscape.

"Ibiza?" I said. "Oh, that's original."

"Might as well. It's a parallel world."

Maya's favorite line flashed to mind.

"Yeah, we should be here for real, when we make our first million," I said.

I navigated to the middle of the room. The Prof. and Krish followed me. Krish reached out to initiate contact.

"You don't need to do that. I already have your feed from the FishEye, remember?" I said, "And you're on speaker phone here."

"Force of habit," he said.

"Didn't you scan the whole room?" I asked, turning to change my field of view. "I can only see part of it."

"No, we have to use only the real-time model from the FishEye. This facility needs clearance for a detailed model."

"So," I said, "what is Project Drone, and how do I fit in."

"Dynamic Robot Operated Neural Entity. I can't give you all the details, Daniel." The Prof. turned to me. "Because most of the project is classified, and even I am not privileged to the information... but what I can tell you is that AYREE has been contracted to build and implement an AI system for an unmanned machine, a remotely operated machine." The Prof. pointed to the insignia on the breast pocket of his overalls. "The client is a department of the Government. These drones will be used to assist in homeland security. Advanced AI will be implemented to evaluate courses of action in such situations as threat assessment, bomb diffusion, terrorist scenarios, and in cases of natural calamities."

"What do you mean AI will evaluate?" I asked.

"Good question. Drones will not use AI to take a course of action in all situations. For instance, in a hostage crisis, the AI will evaluate and recommend a line of action based on many factors and data that it will access with speed and efficiency." The Prof. took a sip of water from a bottle. "In situations such as these, time is of the essence, and it would be a waste of this valuable asset should it be left to a committee of humans."

"So AI is going to influence or steer us in the direction of making a decision?" I asked.

"That's the idea. It's up to a real person to green-light a final action."

"I'd prefer to use the term advise rather than influence or steer," Krish said.

"OK, I get it. So drone is not just an acronym. It's a vehicle or robot?"

"We have several designs for the drones. It's the intelligence part we are working on at this time."

"In what capacity do I contribute?"

"You've already contributed a good deal, Daniel," said Prof. Kumar. "Mr. Singh wants one thing from you–ideas."

"Oh!"

"We were looking at an unmanned all-purpose vehicle based drone with an onboard computer running the AI before."

"Until, our demo!" Krish couldn't hold back.

"Yes. Mr. Singh is now convinced that the ideal drone is not a machine with AI but a human with Wizer augmented intelligence," the Prof. said.

"I'm sure the demo that had him sold on the idea was the FFT upgrade," Krish said.

I moved to a table with four chairs and sat facing the Prof. and Krish.

"Would you like to work on the DRONE project?" asked

Prof. Kumar. "We'd like you to stay here and brainstorm ideas along with perfecting the current modules for the Wizer."

"I have to admit this is an offer I can't refuse," I said.

"Congratulations, then, to both of you," said the Prof. "Your project has gone Code Y."

Krish punched the air in victory. "Code Y, Dan, means top priority at AYREE. We have all the lab's resources at our disposal."

"We'll work on clearance for you to visit the actual location, but meanwhile you can work from the AYREE Lab," said the Prof.

"Thank you, Professor Kumar," I said.

"I should be thanking you, Daniel… and Krish."

"I'll be staying the night here, Dan. We can talk later."

"Sounds like a plan Krish. I'll go get something to eat."

"If you're feeling adventurous, try Indian. I'll ask Maya to call you. She can recommend a place."

Try Indian… hmm. We disconnected. At the far side of the room, the two gentlemen from DRONE were drinking tea. I waved goodbye. It was a pleasant day. Maybe it was because it had been a while, a long while, since I'd been elated. I opened the sliding door to the terrace. There was a light wind blowing and the curtains bellowed as they caught the draft. I got a beer from the refrigerator and looked for something to eat. There was nothing and I was too lazy to fry eggs. Pizza sounded good. I grabbed a tin of nuts and headed out to the lounger. Even the cawing of the crows somehow sounded musical. I turned on the CD player. A soothing breeze on my face made me close my eyes. Sipping beer with eyes closed brought out new flavors in the brew. I was happy. That's what it was.

…

I must have been asleep for a while. Why else would someone be ringing the bell in such an incessant manner? The doorbell was followed with thumping. "Hang on; hang on; I'm there," I shouted. I swung the door open. "Maya!"

"You're half naked, and you take so long to open the door. Where is she?" Maya teased.

"What you doing here?" I said.

"I heard someone was in the mood for Indian," she teased.

"Yeah, I'd love to nibble on something spicy," I said.

She shoved a packed box in my hands. "Here. Enjoy."

"Krish called you?"

"Yeah, he told me to phone and recommend some places for you eat."

"I'm glad you decided to do a house call," I said, putting the box of food on the table and pulling her to me.

"Oh… someone's not had any for some time, I can tell."

"Uh-huh, been a while," I said. We didn't speak another word. I almost ripped off her T-shirt. She put her thumbs into the sideband of her track-pants and pulled them half way off. She wasn't wearing underwear. I was a tad disappointed. I loved wrappers. I watched her wiggle out of her tracks.

"Outdoors," she whispered in my ears, as she slipped my shorts off and ran her hand between my thighs. Maya could turn me on with a single word uttered at the right moment. The exhibit she was gliding her finger nails on was evidence enough. She pushed me down on the lounger.

I looked up at her face. The evening sun was behind her, and her hair highlighted a golden brown. I could feel the cool air on us. I felt the goose flesh on her back and ran my fingertips over the sides of her arms. Goosebumps all over.

She liked that. Her eyes were closed, and there was a smile on her face. A barely audible moan escaped her lips at intervals. She opened her eyes and looked down at me. There was a hint of mischief when she bit her lip. A stream of cool beer made contact with my skin. My stomach instinctively tightened and before I could protest, her lips were on my skin. She kissed slow at first, and then I could hear her making deliberate slurpy noises as she followed the beer stream lower.

We held hands, her fingers between mine. I pulled her to me, and she wrapped her arms and legs around me. Our breathing was in sync; she exhaled as I inhaled.

Maybe that's what they called making love?

We must have dozed off, because we laughed under our breath realizing the entire CD had looped through and the same song was playing again. It was getting a bit chilly; the sun was long gone.

"What time is it?" she murmured. "I should call home, or mom will start to worry."

I picked my phone from the floor. "Six-ish. Don't go."

"You horny bastard."

"No, don't go. I mean stay… forever." I said.

She lifted herself and looked at me, not quite believing what she heard. I couldn't quite believe what I'd said either.

"Dan… are you saying you–"

"Don't say anything," I said pulling her to me and kissing her on the lips. We held each other for a few minutes.

"It's getting cold here," she said and stood. "I'm going in-side."

"Yeah," I said and followed her.

She went into the bathroom, and I could hear the shower run. I was still in a daze. Too much was happening. I didn't quite know if I was actually complaining or happy. It was too much… too fast. I was used to long spells of bad luck, so when anything good happened, I suppose I didn't know how to savor the feeling. We were starving. Maya heated the box of food she'd got, while I took a quick shower. When I came out, there was an aroma that made my mouth water. Indian food had that effect. She was wrapped in one of my oversized towels and setting the table. I couldn't resist sneaking up be-hind her and tugging the towel off. She turned around and almost got blinded by my phone camera flash going off.

"Souvenir of my first lay in India," I said.

She flipped me the birdie.

"Get us some beer," she said. "It goes well with the mint

bread." She didn't bother picking up the towel. Despite being hungry a few minutes ago, I found myself salivating for her more than the food.

"Eat!" she scolded.

"I'm ready for dessert," I said.

We managed to wipe out all the food in about ten minutes flat, though I was sniffling from the spice. She picked up her beer and headed to the bedroom.

"What's up?" I said.

"Mind if I use your laptop?"

"Go ahead."

I followed her. It was an erotic sight, watching her sit naked at my desk. "Get that out of my face, you perv," she said.

"I need to get this. It's every geek's dream to have a naked girl sitting at a computer."

"Don't you dare post it online," she said.

"Awww… not even if I mosaic out your face? That dumbbell needs an audience," I said, pointing to the stud heaving as she breathed. I imagined an invisible pixie there in the middle of a workout.

"Whatcha doing?" I asked. She tapped away at the keyboard and subconsciously smiled at the screen.

"Changing my social status."

"Huh?"

She turned the screen to me. It read: "Relationship Status: In a relationship" and I was tagged in it. My eyes widened in alarm.

"You know how I feel about you, what are you so afraid of?" she said.

"My way of life. I'm afraid of driving you away. Of maybe losing you," I said.

"I understand what you're going through in your life. The uncertainty, the ups and downs… and the only thing I want is to be there for you anyway I can." She caught her breath. "And no, I'm not being a martyr. I know what's in it for me… You. You make me feel alive. You… you, with all your silliness and dreams and stubbornness and determination… that spirit of yours is what motivates me to go on and not give up in my struggles, even this." She pointed to her ankle, and the limp.

"Maya…" I said, walking towards her.

She brushed my hand away as I reached for her.

"The closest you came today is what you said to me outside on the terrace." She was fighting back tears, I could tell. I pulled her close. She did not resist. We held each other in silence.

"Baby–" I said.

The phone interrupted us. She glanced at the table. I looked at my phone. It was Krish. She walked to it, picked it up and handed it to me. "You should answer it," she said, brushing the back of her hand across her eye. She went into the living- room.

"Hey Krish."

"Great day today, huh? This is the break we were looking

for," started Krish.

"Yeah, it's been quite a day," I said.

"So listen… I've emailed you a schedule for the week ahead with priorities on what we have to work on. "Go through it and send me your thoughts. But tomorrow our day starts early. Eight a.m. at the lab?"

"Yeah, for sure."

"Great. Did Maya call you?"

"Umm… She's right here. Brought over some great Indian food."

"She's at your place?"

"Would you like to speak with her?" I asked.

Maya entered the bedroom. She was dressed and wrestling with her hair, attempting to straighten it with a brush.

"Hi, Krish," she said and waited, nodding while he spoke. "Yes, Mama knows I'm here. She had invited Dan over, but I told her he'd be more comfortable when you're around."

He said something.

Maya nodded again. "She was the one who suggested I carry food here."

I could hear him but could not tell what he was saying. He didn't sound angry from the tone of his voice.

"Yes I'm about to leave now to get ready. Don't worry. I'll take a call-taxi." She handed the phone to me.

"Hey, Krish, should I drop Maya?"

"No, it's fine. She'll be OK. Hope you enjoyed the food."

"The best," I said.

"See you," he said, and killed the connection.

"Let me drop you?" I said.

"No, it's not that late, and besides, taxis are right outside the campus," she said, running her fingers through her disheveled hair. Krish is due back the day after tomorrow. You want to drop in?"

"I'd love to," I said.

We held each other. Maya put her fingers to her lips and touched them to mine. "Later."

She left, closing the door behind her.

CHAPTER FIVE

I ARRIVED EARLY AT the Lab. The two men from DRONE were already on their second round of tea, judging by the number of empty Styrofoam cups next to them.

"Good morning, Mr. Daniel"

"Morning," I said. "I need to get me some of that."

The tea machine had a milky mix of the beverage with cardamom, and one cup was never enough. I set things up at my end and waited for Krish.

He called at exactly eight.

"Are we still in Ibiza?" I asked.

"Yeah, same place. It's our world before some regulatory agency takes over and dictates where we can set up virtual shop."

I logged in and found myself in the same white room. Krish was alone."Where's the Prof?"

"He's in a meeting with the Mr. Singh and the board. All board members need to be apprised," he said. "Listen, before we start, I need to ask you something."

I was afraid that would come up.

"Is it serious between you and Maya?"

I feigned innocence with a quizzical look on my face. It was futile. He wasn't looking at my Dirrogate. His Wizer was still in his hands.

"You mean her social status update?" I said.

"Yes… you want to tell me about it?"

"It's complicated," I said. "Can we talk about it later in private?" I tilted my head indicating the other men.

"Fine," he said.

"So I went through the list you sent me, and I did some brainstorming last night," I said.

He put on his Wizer and turned around to locate me. He saw my face mapped to my Dirrogate.

"Let's switch to VOIP. It's secure." He transferred our call to the app. I put my phone down and started the virtual whiteboard to flick through some sketches. "This is an idea I came up with for a drone. We use our FishEye with a laser head on a Quad helicopter."

"For scoping out an area?" he asked.

"Yes. The Quad can stream the data to a mobile command and control center, which in turn relays it to a human operative wearing the Wizer. This way the operative has a pre-built map of the area he is entering and fewer surprises."

"Hmm… I see. Go on."

"This would work well for rescue operations," I said, "and in using Quads, we cut expenses if they are damaged or shot down."

"I'm sure Mr. Singh would like your idea. Reduces the cost of building drones," he said.

"What we have to work on with AYREE engineering is how many sensors we can pack in on a single Quad and still have maneuverability."

"Yes," he said. "The FishEye can be optimized a little more, using lightweight plastics. I'm more concerned about the laser head."

"That's only needed if we want an accurate 3D model for strategic purposes. Otherwise the depth extracted from the stereo FishEye should suffice," I said. "The one important thing we need engineering to scratch their heads over is silencing the rotors."

"Let me file these sketches and notes for the Prof," he said.

My phone rang. It was Kelly.

"You can answer it," Krish said, after I let it ring for a while.

I picked it up. "Hi, can I call you back a little later?" I listened. "No, Kelly, I'm not avoiding you. I'll call this afternoon?" She had hung up but I had to pretend. "Oh, OK. Later… bye."

"Who's Kelly?"

"A friend from back home."

"Oh," he said.

I looked at the screen and knew there was some explaining to do other than my sketches. "Should we maintain connection?" I asked.

"No, I've got a lot of work up to do on my algorithms," he said. "Let's connect later. I assume you're around campus?"

"Yes. Are you back home tomorrow?"

"I hope to be," he said, "but if the Prof. likes the Quad idea, maybe he'll have me on overtime."

"Should we be talking incentives with them?"

"I'm thinking stock options as well," he said.

"Good idea."

"Ideas are your department," he said.

He flashed me a V sign and took the Wizer off. I removed mine and disconnected. There was still time to get more addictive cardamom tea. I carried a full cup down to the campus grounds. It was a bright day, and the slight breeze was inviting. The bench where I first met the Prof. virtually, was in the shade of the tree that we had modeled in the demo simulation. Its real beauty was peta pixels apart from the crude geometry we'd used. Satish and the environment artists would beg to differ. I'd seen their work on the grass and turf in the cricket module.

…

I had to call Kelly!

"So you found time for me?"

"I'm sorry, Kelly. So much has happened I don't quite know where to start."

"Are you coming back anytime soon to our little business opp?"

"Yes. I want to," I said. "I'm involved in a project here. It's both challenging and fascinating. That's what's keeping me booked."

"Does it get over soon?" she asked, "or have you moved there?"

"It will be over sooner or later, and yes I do want to come back to our business plans."

"But?" she said, sensing I was stalling.

In a sheepish tone I replied, "Err… I'm also kind of involved with someone."

"Dear Daniel… pussy is your weakness, isn't it."

I took it in good humor. Her voice was more teasing than nasty. "It's a little more than a one-night thing," I replied.

"Good we didn't have a one-night thing. You'd make me feel like a hooker," she said.

"No! I don't mean it like that."

"I'm joking, silly," she said. "I'm happy for you. Are you still interested in the business side of things back here?"

"I am." I said. "Give me some time to settle in with this project, and then I'll work in parallel on ours."

"OK."

"Hey, look on the bright side," I said, "You don't have to draw out any sexual harassment clauses now."

We laughed.

"Speak to you later, Dan. Take care of yourself."

...

As it turned out, the Prof. greenlit the idea of the Quad as the drone. It would be augmented by a human operative. Krish remarked that many of his colleagues thought the speed at which finance was getting sanctioned for the project was unusual. It really was Code Y at AYREE.

For the next few days, my Dirrogate and I worked at virtual DRONE headquarters. The white room was a mesh draped over a beach in the real world, somewhere in Ibiza. Krish was not authorized to tell me where the real DRONE HQ was until I got clearance from the government.

"It's not something like a nuclear facility or anything," he said, "It's government red-tape more than anything that prevents you from being here."

Our digital surrogate solution worked out fine. The Prof. and Krish said it was as though I stood in the room. The only thing they wanted to improve on was the fit of the Wizer for wearer comfort. I spent most of the day at the lab and returned to the apartment and my bed only to sleep.

"Tomorrow we celebrate," Arjun said, speaking to my Dirrogate. He was at DRONE headquarters with the Prof. and Krish.

"Mr. Singh has invited us all to the club," said the Prof. "It's also payday." Krish raised his hand for a high-five. My Dirrogate responded.

On the day the Quad arrived, while we were assembling it, Krish said we needed a face-to-face talk. I knew what he had in mind and tried to worm my way out with a joke about a man-to-avatar talk.

"This isn't a time to joke, Dan," he said.

"Yes, Krish… Maya and I are in a relationship," I said. "I was unsure, but I'm not anymore. We are in a relationship."

He was being a protective elder brother to her, but he realized he was also up against headstrong Maya. She had told me that she reminded him it was her life.

"Are you in love with her?" he asked.

"That's a private matter between us," I reasoned with him. "But for what it's worth… I'll be truthful to Maya and never hurt her."

…

We were traveling to the club in style. Mr. Singh had sent his chauffeur-driven limo to fetch each of us. When I entered the limo, Krish and Maya were already in.

"Well, congrats you two," Maya said. "Does this mean you'll be staying a while?"

"I'll have to think about it," I said, turning to her with a wink.

The vehicle slowed down.

"There already?" I asked.

"No, I'd asked the driver to make a stop. Won't be long."

"Not now…" Maya started to protest.

"It's fine. I'm OK with waiting," I said.

Maya looked at me and then at him. "Oh alright, hurry."

Krish got out of the limo.

"Where's he gone?" I asked.

"It's kind of a thing he does… something of a tradition from Dad."

"Oh… I didn't know."

"Dad always believed that when good fortune came your way, you shared it with the less fortunate. Whenever Dad used to get a raise or bonus, he used to go to one of these charities to make a donation."

"The sign says cerebral palsy and special needs institute," I said, peering out of the window at a dilapidated building.

"Yes, Dad's sister was born with the condition. It was a financial strain on his family taking care of her." She took a deep breath. "Dad's always told Krish that his God given gift of intelligence should also be used to help those less fortunate. He wanted Krish to spend time helping with research in this field."

"God given… and what about you, Maya?" I turned to

face her. "You were there, heck we both were, on that horrible day when he was taken in. Do you think your Dad should suffer the way he is?"

"Let's not go there, Dan."

"Why? Because it's taboo to question?" I turned away and stared out the window. "You know, I'm not wrong on this... bad things happen to good people. I refuse to believe that there's eternal happiness someplace else."

"Let's forget about everything and have a nice time this evening," she said. "You're here; I'm here; it's rare that we get to be together."

I leaned in, and she met me halfway. When our lips touched, I felt something beautiful in our kiss. The moment lingered, neither of us breaking away.

"Krish is coming." Maya gestured toward the building.

I sat back and fidgeted with my seat belt.

"Sorry 'bout that. Hope I didn't take too long."

"Not at all," I said.

We drove past Study Street. A few teenagers were lighting a campfire. "Every night, huh?" I asked, looking in their direction. Krish nodded.

"Maybe we should get AYREE to donate a few slates to them?" I said, pointing to a group of about five boys who could not have been more than 12 or 13 years. He strained to look, but the limo had turned the corner and Study Street was behind us.

"We're almost there," Maya said.

The limo turned and entered a side road and then into a

gated compound. There was a large open ground used as a parking lot and three buildings. The area appeared to be an abandoned industrial complex. It was Saturday and the open ground outside the main entrance was filled with cars of all makes. This was the club where the high-profile people of the city wanted to be seen on a Saturday night. The gate charge was unaffordable to the average club goer. I wondered how many rich people lived in this city of contrasts, if the crowd lined up was the weekend turnout at just one night-club. Even the rich had to queue up when there were too many of them. The part I liked best was the sound of the metal clasp clicking to let us in. A privilege and a high. The quizzical look on the people in line was always priceless. They must wonder how much richer you were. As we neared the club's entryway, I rolled down the window and heard the familiar thump of bass speakers. A guard came towards us and signaled us to halt. People in the queue turned to look at us. The driver opened his door and said something to him. The guard promptly saluted and waved to one of the valets who came running.

"V.I.P. treatment?" I looked toward Maya.

"You could get used to it, huh?" She smiled.

"I could you know!" I said, offering her my arm in exaggerated chivalry and slinging my backpack over my shoulder.

"Behave, both of you," he said.

Maya laughed and linked her arm in mine, as we walked to the door. People in line were waiting their turn to get in, but the guard released the clasp on the velvet barricade and ushered us inside. It was a sizable club, a warehouse converted into a nightspot to be exact. The DJ cabin at the far end was at quite a height from the sunken dance floor.

A sea of heads were bobbing to the beat. House music was playing. An arm brushed against me and I turned to look.

"I'm sorry. I missed my step," a woman said, as she walked by. "Did you see that?" I turned to Maya, smiling.

"Yeah I saw the *run-dee*," she said and curled her lip, feigning disgust.

"I love when you go all native!" I grinned.

Maya punched me on my arm.

Krish was ahead of us looking out for Arjun. A waiter approached Krish and said something. Krish leaned in closer to hear him over the booming bass. Then he turned to us and waved us to follow. We circled the dance floor and walked up the stairs to the higher level. I could swear my neck was made of rubber. Maya punched me in the arm every time I turned to look at one of those raven haired beauties. How could there be so many single hot looking women in one place? What was it that the men in the city were doing wrong? We reached a table where it was quieter, and there sat Arjun and his father. The Prof. with them. Mr. Singh was holding a lit cigar. A plume of smoke rose up from the tip that randomly caught a stray beam of laser light. The caramel coffee odor was not unpleasant, and I found myself taking deeper breaths to sample its fragrance. Arjun stood and came towards us. He knew how to carry off a cream colored suit.

"Hi, Krish, Dan. Welcome, welcome. You're looking lovely, Maya." He lifted and kissed the back of her hand.

She smiled.

"Dad, the lovely lady is Krish's sister, Maya."

"Good to meet you all," he said.

"Likewise, Mr. Singh," I said. "Good evening, Professor."

The Prof. acknowledged all of us with a handshake. We sat at the table. There was a chair short, and Arjun stood and pulled one from another table. He wedged it in between where Maya and I were sitting.

"Would you like anything, sir?" enquired a waiter, bowing low near Mr. Singh.

The elder Singh gestured towards us.

"I'll have beer," Krish said.

"Same for me, please," I said.

"I'll have a bottle of sparkling water, please," said the Prof.

"Get a bottle of your best white wine," Arjun said. "Or would you prefer some champagne, Maya?"

He was making me ruin the soles of my expensive shoes with my toe nails. Why was I getting all territorial? A few minutes ago I was looking around at other women.

Maya smiled. "A glass of white wine is fine, Arjun. Thanks."

"A refill for sir?" The waiter gestured with the open palm of his hand to Arjun's and his father's nearly empty glasses.

Mr. Singh nodded. "A round of champagne too."

"I hope you're being treated well, Daniel?"

"Yes, quite well," I said. "Thank you."

"We always treat important guests well," he said, then smiled and raised his glass for a last gulp. "I have a little while; then I have to go attend to business with some of my guests." He pointed to a another cordoned of VIP seating area some distance away from us.

Another waiter brought a tray of champagne flutes.

"To us!" We clinked our glasses. Even the Prof. had a sip in keeping with the spirit and returned his glass to the tray.

"Why don't you all enjoy the hospitality of the club, while I finish some discussions with Professor Kumar?" Mr. Singh said.

Arjun turned to me. "Would you like to do a guest session?"

"Itching to try this baby out." I flexed my fingers - the three finger glove, whirred to life.

We made our way through the mass of bodies. It was a full night with at least a thousand people, I estimated. Arjun introduced me to the DJ who let me plug in my hard drive. I decided to stand and get a feel of the vibe. It was a new audience. I looked around and spotted Krish walking up to the cabin. Maya and Arjun headed to the dance floor. So that's what the bastard had in mind!

The DJ was playing an Indian track that was popular, judging by the way the crowd moved. It had a high pitched but melodious female vocal over a steady beat. With a smile, he invited me to take over. I was entering the zone. It could have been the champagne and beer. I searched for a back beat that would fit the current song and cued it in, slowly easing up on the fader. The DJ heard it coming through and nodded to the beat. It was risky... one wrong move, and I would lose the dance floor. The club's cabin was state of the art; each deck had its own EQ stack. He knew what I was looking for. He pointed it out above the mixer. I slowly started killing the lower frequencies on the record and ramped up the volume on my backbeat. The female singers Hindi vocals were riding smoothly atop the hip hop bass line and drums. The crowd noticed. The DJ noticed. He gave me a thumbs-up.

I had the Wizer on. It was linked to the glove... cuing back her vocals and plugging them into the mix was easy with my fingers on auto-pilot. The crowd went wild when they heard what appeared to a popular phrase in the song coming in over a heavy kick drum and fretless bass slide. I looked again at the dance floor. The mix was going down well with the crowd. I looked around for Maya. She was... or was it Arjun? I couldn't say, but one of them was too close to the other, and they were both moving in sync.

I asked the DJ for any other popular track and was handed another Indian single.

I put the record on the platter and wore the headset. The label read in bold: "Chura Liya." It had a good backbeat. A little tweak of pitch with my index finger, and it glided into the mix. The crowd went berserk when they identified the tune. I hadn't heard that track before, but it grew on me right from the first few bars. Krish was talking to someone at his table. I looked at the floor again. Maya was sipping another glass of champagne on the floor and was really moving with Arjun. If she was getting drunk, she needed to stop. If she was trying to tell me something, I was hearing her loud and clear.

The track was nearing it's end and I was back-spinning the next one in, when it happened... The unmistakable sound of gunshots! BLAM!! BLAM!! BLAM!!

I leaned in and ripped the needle off the vinyl. Two men burst into the cub from a service entrance. The one behind, I recognized as a club Bouncer. He was dressed in black. He sprinted to the stage and up onto the DJ cabin ledge. He had a vantage point. I saw him leveling his weapon, taking aim – taking too long to aim – The man in front, spun around, marked and fired! BLAM!

Open target. The Bouncer crashed down, breaking the low glass barricade and falling onto the mixing desk. People screamed. Krish who was at the cabin door, and the DJ, stood stunned. We all were in shock. The killer...the Terrorist, grabbed a woman on the dance-floor and put his gun to her head, using her as a human shield. Nobody in the club moved. Two Bouncers on the upper level had their handguns trained on him. The Terrorist fired a warning shot at the ceiling and swiftly put the gun back at the woman's head. The Bouncers lowered their weapons near their feet. People around the dance-floor instinctively dropped to their knees, cowering. Some near the entrance, ran.

The Terrorist scanned the area, he did a double take

when he saw Arjun. In a flash the Terrorist pushed the woman away and took up position behind Arjun, pointing his gun at Arjun's head. I hard Krish's audible gasp as we realized Maya was standing only a few yards away from Arjun. The Terrorist realized that Maya was with Arjun, and looked at her and back at his hostage. He stayed with Arjun. I saw Mr. Singh come to the edge of the rail, on the upper level, gripping it with both hands, looking helpless. The Terrorist knowing he now was the only one armed, swung his arm around in an arc – a warning. People on the dance-floor backed away, clearing a path toward the entrance.

I looked at Krish. His eyes went wide as realized what I was doing. Inch by inch the Mesh Arm Cast came into view as I rolled the sleeve of my T-shirt higher. Krish mouthed a silent "NO" and nodded his head from side to side, slowly at me. I reached out gingerly and slid the dead Bouncer's handgun which was lying on the mixer, toward me. As I watched, yellow circles, contorted and conformed to the outline of the gun, hugging it's contours. In a couple of seconds, they turned green. Identified: '0.22 Beretta' got overlaid in my field of view. I darkened the Wizers tint a few notches. The Terrorist was getting ready to make an exit. He moved his arm with the gun, beckoning Maya to follow them. Maya did not move.

I picked up the dead Bouncer's handgun. It still felt a little warm to the touch where it made contact with the uncovered palm of my right hand. I felt the metal click as the three finger glove connected with the gun. My thumb, encased in the glove, moved off it's own accord, driven by the exoskeleton glove. Safety Catch – check; Uncock hammer. The Terrorist was losing his patience with Maya. He grunted at her with his gun, forcing it against Arjun's temple as a threat. I reached out with my left hand and pressed down on the recessed activation button on my right shoulder. My right arm went rigid. I tapped on the temple of the Wizer...twice. My entire view of the club got drained off color. Everything was now a live grayscale depth map. Two graphic outlines – Human ghosts, flew out into the club; one red, one blue. The digital surrogate ghosts attached and conformed to the Arjun and the the Terrorist. Four glowing dots locked onto the red dirrogate – the Terrorist. His body was painted with a heat-map of color patches from red, green and yellow.

Blink to Select FFT, came up in my field of view. I blinked my eyes, holding my eyelids shut for a second then opened them. The internal facing camera of the Wizer understood the command. Color returned to the when my eyes re-opened. Blink to Select: IK Movement Odds: NODE 1 - Head 60%, NODE 2 - Shoulder 20%, NODE 3 - Occluded, NODE 4 - Wrist 70%

I moved my head. Yellow gun-sight crosshairs jumped and locked onto Node 1... for a split second. I shook my head. The crosshairs disengaged. The Terrorist looked at the DJ cabin seeing me with the Wizer on, and realizing those were not regular sunglasses. He hesitated and frowned. The crosshairs locked onto Node 2. I blinked. The target turned green. My arm lifted and pointed straight out. The Terrorist recovered, realizing what was happening and trained his gun at the cabin. My index finger squeezed. Once. BLAM!!

He was lifted a couple of feet off the ground and he crashed down to the floor. Then...

the EXPLOSION! Followed by an aftershock that traveled through our bodies. Glass rained on the floor. Everyone was frozen in shock. Before we could react, there was a gunshot. We couldn't tell from which direction it came.

Then… the stampede.

People ran for the entrance. More gunshots behind us. I dashed down to the floor, grabbed Maya as she was running toward the cabin, and we ran towards the main door. Stay calm was not an easy rule to follow when a human tsunami was headed your way. I turned left and saw a woman screaming as people trampled her. No one stopped.

Maya looked at me and yelled, “It's no use! Let's go.”

I looked back at the woman again. Another shot rang out. Then my legs gave way as if kicked by an elephant at the back of my knees. My face hit the tiled floor and I tasted blood in my mouth. I looked up and saw Maya a few steps ahead of me, her arms flailing, trying to make her way through the crowd running against her.

“Dan!” she screamed.

I looked behind me to determine the cause of my excruciating pain. A part of the overhead light truss had crashed down on my legs, pinning me to the floor.

“Go, Maya!” I yelled as shoes and heels dug into my

back. I cowered and covered my head with my hands. My cheek was pressed to the floor and at that angle I could see the woman's eyes... staring at me. Another pair of shoes crushed her glasses into the bridge of her nose. A stream of blood poured from her nostril. Her lifeless eyes were still wide open. Maya jumped on me, shielding me with her body. She screamed again as more people trampled us. There was a volley of gunfire and I saw someone fall a couple of yards in front of us. People started running the other way. We were spared.

"Maya!" I heard Krish calling from above. "Maya, Maya." I could hear him pound down the stairs.

I strained my head to look around. My vision was fuzzy, but I saw the Prof. and Mr. Singh and Arjun and uniformed police standing around us. I felt Maya's heaving body on me. Thank God she was alive. Her hand was on top of my head. Arjun shouted to the bouncers in Hindi. The truss was lifted off me. I freed my arm from under my chest and turned to her.

"Maya, No!" I heard an unearthly scream from Krish as he ran toward us. "She's been shot!"

It took an eternity for me to register what he said.

"Call the fucking ambulance!" he cried out. "Don't just stand there!"

We heard the siren outside. Two paramedics rushed towards us. I reached out to hold Maya.

"Don't touch her," one of the paramedics shouted.

I flopped back. Maya hadn't said a word. Her eyes and

mouth were open, and her body was heaving with every breath she took.

One of the paramedics said to the other, "There's no sign of an exit wound. It could still be lodged inside."

She looked at me and in a faint voice said, "Dan."

I crawled to her and held her face in my hand, tears rolling down both our faces.

"I love you," she said. "Know that. I..."

I put my fingers to her mouth. "Shhh… don't say anything, baby."

Before I could say another word, she let out a shrill cry as the paramedics lifted her onto a stretcher. Krish ran alongside them. Another pair of paramedics arrived at the scene and checked me. I couldn't feel my feet, only a numbing sensation as though a million pins were embedded in my legs.

"You said no one would get hurt," a loud distorted voice broke the silence.

The police unholstered their weapons and were training them on someone. I craned my neck and looked around despite the sharp pain. Professor Kumar had a handgun aimed at Mr. Singh.

"Put down your weapon, or we will fire," said one of the senior uniformed officers. The Prof. was trembling with the gun in his hand. "You said no one will get hurt," he kept repeating, his voice choking. The officers took position behind him and one of them jumped at the gun while another tackled him to the floor. At the same time, on the other side, an officer dove at Mr. Singh to get him out of the way. An officer kicked the gun, sending it spinning under a bar-stool

"He's responsible for this." The Prof. was pointing to Mr. Singh.

"I don't know what happened here, but all of you are needed for questioning," said the senior officer.

The paramedics gave me a shot, carried me on another stretcher and made their way to the door.

"Where's Maya?" I asked.

"That ambulance has left, sir. She needs emergency treat-ment."

Outside, as they hauled me into the ambulance, I got a glimpse of the aftermath of the explosion that we heard and felt earlier. A single story building in the same complex had caved in. The previous ground floor had imploded on itself and was no more. In it's place was the crumpled top section. Firefighters were hosing down a small fire, and a few dam-aged cars were being removed by a forklift. My vision was going blurry. The painkiller was taking effect. As paramedics hoisted the stretcher into the back of the ambulance, I saw the distinct shape of a woman walk up. I tried to lift my head. She stood in front of me and came closer. All I could see was a pair of blurry red lips. The ambulance doors shut and the siren wailed. On the way to the hospital, the only thing I could think of was Maya. Providence, it seemed, had de-clared war on me.

...

When I opened my eyes, I found myself looking at a patch of mold on the corner wall of my room in the hospital. The painkillers I was given must have worn off, because the pain in the back of my right knee was excruciating. A doctor was standing near me, preparing a syringe. "I'm going to give you another shot to ease the pain, Daniel."

I could only nod and forced a half smile.

"Where is Maya?" I asked, hoping that he would somehow give me a redeeming answer.

"She's in the ICU, Daniel," said the doctor. "You have some visitors."

He beckoned the nurse to open the door. It was the Prof. and the senior police officer from the night before.

"Daniel, I'm truly sorry this has happened," said the Prof.

I only stared at him, holding my face expressionless.

"We have to ask you some questions, Daniel," said the officer in a solemn voice. He took off his cap and held it under his arm. "We'll wait however, seeing you're under the influence of pain-killers."

"Tell me about Maya," I said.

"Maya's in intensive care. She has a bullet in her right side near her rib cage and doctors are working on it. She's unconscious, is all we know," said the officer.

"Krish?"

"He's OK and with her, Daniel," said the Prof.

"I need to see her now," I said getting up. Something snapped, and I collapsed back on the bed.

The nurse came running. "You can't move. Your leg–"

"She's unconscious, Daniel, and in critical condition," said the Prof. "Even Krish is not allowed in. He will call me if there is a change."

The police officer put on his cap and left.

I winced in pain. "What happened back there?"

The Prof. pulled a chair to sit beside me. "Mr. Singh has these friends. He showed them the Wizer and was offered a lot to have a consignment made for them." The Prof. cleared his throat. "But they wanted a demo first. The collapsed building was a warehouse owned by Mr. Singh."

"It didn't just collapse did it?" I asked, "It was a controlled demolition by experts."

"Yes it was," said the Prof. "Only the expert in this case was a drone."

I lifted myself by my elbows, leaning forward. "I don't understand."

"These friends of Mr. Singh... they belong to a known terrorist cell." Prof. Kumar shifted in his chair, his voice dry. "The demo of the Wizer and drone was to place explosives at precise locations in the warehouse to blow it up. It would serve two purposes: Mr. Singh could claim insurance on the goods stocked in there," he went on, "and the demo would show the precision possible in strikes involving a drone."

Something was not making sense. "I don't get it. How can a Quad place explosives? Do you already have an articulated robot drone?"

"No, Daniel. The drone was from an idea that you gave."

"Me? What idea?"

"A Human Drone... A person controlled by remote. Singh called the terrorist that, during his confession. The drone, Daniel," said the Prof, "was a person who'd taken a suicide pledge."

I noticed Prof. Kumar's fingers were trembling. He placed one hand over the other. "I was told that the drone would be human, I was told this would be a simulation and I did not know the explosives would be real, much less that it was a suicide mission. The real demolition expert was in a vehicle outside the club compound."

"There wasn't even the need for a Quad to stream a live view of the warehouse in that case," I said, after I comprehended the macabre plot.

The Prof. nodded. "The drone got through security because he was receiving live instructions and answers from his supervisor; the drone operator. The Wizer already had a map pre-programmed with the structural makeup of the warehouse."

I listened in horror, realizing what was possible with the Wizer.

"It superimposed all the wiring, pipelines and locations that the drone had to go and place the explosives at," said the Prof. "With the Wizer, it was like having X-ray vision. This made our otherwise illiterate drone, a demolition expert."

"He was supposed to get buried in there?" I asked.

"Yes that was his oath. To first get rid of the Wizer, then activate the timed explosive belt."

"Why would a person do that?" It was all so incredulous.

"Money for his family. Enough to put food on their table and send his children to school for a few years. Every year people take their lives here, Daniel. People with debts, people with no motivation to live… These terror cells offer them an exit policy: death benefits to the rest of the family."

"It all went wrong, didn't it?" I said, knowing the answer beforehand.

"The suicide bomber changed his mind at some point and made a call to the operator that the Wizer was disposed of, but while he was saying a final prayer that the operator was waiting on, he must have activated and removed the explosive trigger belt he was wearing and taken cover."

The Prof. helped himself to a bottle of water from the side table. His hands trembling, he took a long gulp. "Immediately after the explosion, the bomber ran through the kitchen of the club. You know the rest."

"While you merely injured him, a Bouncer at the club shot the drone down during the gunfight that followed. Mr. Singh did not tell me who the client really was."

"Mr. Singh has testified to my innocence, but we both are still under an arrest warrant," said the Prof. "AYREE has posted a bond for me, but it will be for a judge to decide the outcome. We've also testified that you and Krish have no involvement or knowledge of this plan." The Prof. gulped down the rest of the water. "You are not under arrest but will be required to give a statement at the station. AYREE's internal investigation is uncovering involvement of Mr. Singh with a group in East Europe."

"East Europe?"

"Some guests of Mr. Singh - foreigners, were arrested trying to leave the country. AYREE board is investigating a possible compromise in the code driving the Exoskeleton Mesh Arm - a backdoor."

"Backdoor... Backdoor..." My head reeled. I was naive in my thinking that the Wizer could only be used one way... to make right what was wrong. "I need to be near Maya," I said... trying to stand again. I gripped the edge of the bed, and realized that the pain was localized to an area behind the knee of my right leg.

"Help me to a wheelchair, please," I said, wincing. "Even if I can't go near her, I need to see her."

The nurse opened the door and called for a wheelchair. We went up the elevator to the ICU on the second floor. Krish and his mother were sitting huddled on a corner couch outside the door. Maya's mother was sobbing, and Krish had his arms around her. As the nurse wheeled me down the corridor towards Krish's mother, there was only one thought running through my mind... what a perverse world we lived in, where the reward for good people was misery... unadulterated misery. It was the second time in less than a year that I saw his mother suffering, her gratuity for being a pious woman. We waited outside that door for any sign that would tell us Maya was improving. None came. After what seemed like hours, a doctor approached.

"She's still not out of her coma," he said. "But if you like you may visit her one at a time. Please be extremely careful about what you say to her," he said, "and talk in a reassuring voice. It may help her in gaining consciousness."

Maya's mother and Krish went in together. He stood behind the door while their mother walked to the bed. I wheeled myself closer to the glass window, seeing Maya for the first time... the first time since she saved my life. I couldn't fight the tears anymore. Her mother couldn't bear to see her in that state. She almost slumped by the side of the bed. He ran to her side and helped steady her. He took her to the door, and the nurse helped her to the sofa. Krish held the door open, and I wheeled myself in.

I put my hands on the steel side rail of the bed. The tips of my fingers barely touched her hand. "Maya, I know you want to hear me... please hear me. I love you. I'll always love you."

Every part of me wanted to ditch my existing assumptions about God and life. I begged for a miracle. I wanted to see her stir. Any sign would save my soul, would make me believe, I reasoned. But it was the real world wasn't it? Miracles must happen only in some parallel universe.

...

The hospital bed was not comfortable, but that might have been due to the position I had to sleep in. The pain was at the back of my knee, where the truss beam had pinned me. I awoke many times from the painkiller induced sleep. At one time it was to replay the stampede in my head. The face of the woman who got trampled came to haunt me. If I had not hesitated, perhaps Maya would not be in the ICU. It was the open eyes and lifeless face as the woman was being stepped on that looked down at me from the white ceiling. The TV cast an eerie blue glow around the room that colored her face if I blinked. I switched off the TV and looked out the window. Lights were going off in the city one at a time like oil lamps burning out. Burned out people, working hard to make a living. Some even willing to give up their lives so their children could eat. I had to wonder what sadistic pleasure and entertainment human suffering must provide to the divine game players who decided the fate of their pawns in a board game they made of life.

...

I must have aroused the wrath of the powers that be that night, but I refused to give them the pleasure of reveling in my pain with the news that came from the ICU the next morning.

Maya was no more.

The doctor came to my room, and gave me another merciful shot to ease the burden. But truth be told, at that moment I was numb to pain, physical or otherwise. Something died in me on the day I witnessed her funeral pyre burn. She was dressed in white and I looked on as the red and orange flames rose to obscure, engulf and claim her. Her mother and Krish were inconsolable.

With a crutch I stood there, looking on as the fire burned

and then died out and people left. I stood there, handicapped. There was no reason left to stay. For once I wanted to go to the place I would later come to love as my real home. The police insisted on a statement as part of protocol, so I had to go to the station. The board members of AYREE, all influential in their own way along with Prof. Kumar and Mr. Singh reiterated that Krish and I were innocent. We were victims of circumstance and had nothing to do with planning, sabotage or aiding manslaughter. As such, no record would be kept on file with the police or at immigration that could tarnish my name in any way.

Mr. Singh was initially sentenced to three years in prison and a hefty fine. He had connections. He was out on bail and appealing the ruling. Prof. Kumar was not charged as an accomplice. Again, it must have been the well connected board members of AYREE that may have influenced the verdict. I was relieved for him. I waited with a single suitcase packed for the taxi to arrive. Ram bhai helped me in, although my leg was getting better, and the pain manageable. I turned to take one last look at the white building as the taxi pulled out of the gates of the campus.

It was time to take back control of my life.

CHAPTER SIX

THE FIRST THING THAT HIT me was the familiar yet peculiar smell of central air-conditioning when I entered the apartment. The concierge was kind enough to ride the elevator up with me and roll in my suitcase when I opened the door. An involuntary shudder ran down my back. I remembered I'd turned the temperature down all the way in the apartment before I'd left. Hobbling to open the slider, I stepped out on the sundeck. Not as spacious as the terrace at the AYREE guesthouse, but the view was still unbeatable. I needed to use the bathroom. I walked to the faucet and let cold water soothe my eyes.

That's when I noticed Maya's toothbrush. There was a stabbing pain at the base of my throat. I waited a few seconds and tried to swallow. It hurt. I went to the closet for a towel, and as I opened the doors, Maya's perfume engulfed me. I closed them and held them shut. I was afraid the scent would get diluted. I needed it trapped in there forever, so I would not forget.

Everywhere I looked, she was there. The AR scope was still at the same angle that she peered through. I could never dare change it. Tears started as I walked around the apartment. A dull pain was returning to my leg. I dug into my backpack and rummaged for pills. In one of the pockets was the envelope. Twenty Thousand Dollars. I remembered her squeezing my hand. Maya had said we should make out on a bed full of those notes, but what I really wanted was to hold her the way I did on that terrace. That would have sufficed. The CD was in my pack. I limped to the server and turned it on. I closed the curtains. Near the couch on the floor was the cushion that we used to share. It still had her scent. The way I used to lift her hair and bury my face in the back of her neck... that was the familiar smell I was breathing in as I pressed the cushion to my face. It muffled my cries.

The Wizer fell out of the bag and onto the carpet. What other kind of evil was it capable of? I needed something to help me sleep. Hard liquor was the only choice.

The painkillers and vodka must have taken effect, or maybe it was exhaustion that claimed me. When I awoke the CD was at the same song that we had made love to, that day in on the terrace. It was evening now and the sky was some shade of reddish purple.

My phone was back on the home network, and the inbox was full of messages and missed calls. The most recent were from Kelly. Krish had called as well as sent me a text message. I didn't know what to say to him if I called. I picked up the Wizer from the floor and turned it on, noticing the high pitched but barely audible whirr as it calibrated itself.

"Network detected: Connect?" was on the see-through display. My fingers punched in the password, and I was connected to the media server. Browsing the playlist on the server brought back a flood of memories. Viewing the clips on the Wizer made for a more intimate experience. Many videos were of us having sex, or was it making love? I only then understood the difference. You called it sex if you were successful at alienating emotion from the act. It was love all along, but nobody told me.

I lay on the couch with my leg propped on a cushion. It was eerie hearing our voices through the Wizer, as I skipped through recordings.

"Stop that, you perv." Maya's voice pierced my ears.

I sat upright. On-screen, the video clip playing was the one I had recorded of Maya while she was fiddling with the AR scope. The clip was only a couple of minutes long. I bolted towards the window and twisted my ankle, forgetting that

I could barely walk. The pain did not matter. I pulled open the curtains, almost ripping them off the rails. It was the same time of day as it was when the recording was made.

I paused the video.

I was looking at the scope in the room through the Wizer, and there she was. Maya's wispy image was looking through the scope! My head tilted of its own accord to match the angle of the old visor through which the clip had been recorded. I adjusted the tint of the Wizer and looped the video.

"Stop that, you perv." played over and over. My head did not move. I sat there watching those few moments of video till my neck hurt.

...

They say time is a great healer; only I wasn't injured. No, I was incensed, possessed with the idea of not letting her go. She was no wound after all. Why should time try to heal me by eroding her from my memory? Over those next few days, I lost track of time itself. I didn't answer any calls, I slept… had I slept? I don't remember. I searched through the server for all the images I had of Maya. There were a lot of photos and some videos that were recorded by the wall mounted FishEye. Those had depth information that I needed. I was meticulous in how I pieced the different angles of Maya's face together to create a 3D point cloud, a digital sculpture of her face. The avatars that Krish and I used for our digital surrogates were simple crude models. They were optimized for real time rendering on smart phones, with the features of our faces mapped as live video. That had sufficed for collaborative work. I wanted Maya to be... real.

If you were to squeeze your eyes shut and picture someone you loved, what kind of image would you come up with? I wanted realism that was far superior to that. As it was, her face was a fragile image, stored in the recesses of my mind's eye. I would not let it deteriorate over time.

It was approximately a week later that Maya's digital surrogate was born.

I woke in the morning and rubbed my eyes as I entered the living room. I wore the Wizer and looked around the apartment. She was sitting with her legs folded on the couch, headphones on, listening to music. Her head swayed gently to the rhythm. I stood there, looking at her. There were so many questions vying for answers. Had I lost my mind? Was I being disrespectful? What were the moral and ethical issues? During all the introspection, only one thing remained constant: my gaze, locked on her.

There was a lot of work to do. So many memories to bring alive I did not know where to begin. Maya liked listening to her classical dance music. Whenever I was working, and she visited, she would curl up on the couch, wear her headphones and immerse herself in her music. It was an easy frame to create. I had worked with no concept of day or night. The stock of energy drinks were rapidly depleting from the refrigerator. I learned what I could about AI from

Internet archives and subscribing to academic research journals. My aim was to revisit the incomplete structures that Krish had begun for the demo. I re-adapted Maya's frame to a model of my apartment. With my understanding of what he had explained and with help from those journals, I created a master for the apartment and populated it with as much as I could think of in terms of navigable paths, entities, furniture. Cosmetic issues dealing with occlusion and interaction macros were standard AR code for me.

When Maya walked to the couch, an automatic macro triggered to make her body naturally transition to the way she loved to sit with her legs folded under her. I looked at her, as she walked toward the window and placed her hands on the pane. She was wearing a white summer dress with a blue floral print. It was a replica of a dress in one of her photographs. It swayed naturally as she moved, testament to how far cloth and physics simulation had come in the graphics industry. We were moving towards more realistic digital replicas of humans. I saw Maya as the next logical evolution.

There was still a lot of work to be done. I would have loved for every little detail to show in the texture of her skin when the sun caught the back of her ears. They had a faint pink glow near the tips. At AYREE, the environment designers called it subsurface scattering. I would need help in creating that level of digital skin for Maya. Satish and his team would be able to handle it, but how was I going to explain it all to Krish?

He would think I had gone mad, or worse, he would be

offended with what I was doing. I picked up the phone. I had to call Krish. I couldn't do it, I dialed Kelly instead.

"Hey, you! You're back?" she asked.

"Hi. Kelly. Yes, I came in a few days ago but had a lot of things to sort out." I didn't wait for her to respond. "There's a lot to tell you. I will in due course. I only wanted to get in touch to say I'm back."

"That's cool," she said. "Is there something bothering you?"

"It's personal, and I'll have to deal with it, but thanks for asking."

"OK. Know that whenever you're settled, and if you're still keen, I am too… for our project."

"I am. I won't be going anywhere soon," I said.

"Give me a call anytime. Dan, take care of yourself."

I looked around the apartment. It was empty. The Wizer was on the coffee table. I put it on and looked around. Maya was by the scope. I stood there in the middle of the room looking at her. It was all wrong on so many counts. I should let her go. Yet as I stood there watching her, against better logic and judgment, I was hoping she would turn around and say "Stop that, you perv," in her playful voice. I could keep adding to the frame's contents… one sample, one rule, one parameter as we went along. This was a parallel universe that we were living in after all. Why couldn't we start from scratch and build it all over, one memory at a time? How different was it from having Maya's lifeless photograph in a frame? Or playing looping videos whenever I was down and missed her? Why couldn't we live our memories to the fullest extent possible. Maybe make new ones? Was that even possible?

I had to call Krish. If he thought I'd gone mad, then at least it would be from someone who'd give me a logical explanation. I realized the reason I didn't ask anyone for advice except him: Others I knew, didn't use logic. They evangelized the catchall phrase, "have faith." The only thing that scared me was that Krish might be so insulted, so outraged at what I was doing, that he would never speak to me again.

I dialed his number.

"Daniel! Where have you been?" he asked. There was concern in his voice.

"I'm at home," I said. "How's your Dad keeping?"

"Dad... Dad passed away three days ago. We had to tell him about... Maybe he couldn't cope, or maybe, it was just his time."

"I'm sorry, Krish. I'm so sorry."

"Thankfully he passed away without suffering. It's been too much for Mom. She's at her sister's."

There was silence. We didn't know what to say.

"I wish you'd stayed. I needed you. You left too soon."

"No! Krish, Maya left too soon. I never got to say goodbye."

"I know, Dan." I heard his voice choke.

"I loved her… I love her," I said.

Both of us broke down.

"The house is empty here…" he stammered. "I play her

classical music in her room, so I can feel she's around."

"I have a CD of her music in the apartment. I played it yesterday," I said. "I'd like you to come here. Ask them for some time off?"

"AYREE is under internal investigation. So all projects–"

" –Not interested in that. What about you? Can't you come?"

"I don't know. Let me think about it."

There was silence again.

"The Prof. is still running the lab and has been to my house at least twice. Not on work calls but simply to sit and have tea. He hasn't forgiven himself," he said. "I've told him it's not his fault. It's God's will."

My fingers dug into the armrest of the couch. The anger in me needed an outlet.

"You're free from AYREE until they sort things, right? And your mom's not there. A change might be good?" I cleared my throat. "I wish you'd come here," I said.

He must have heard the plea in my voice.

"OK, let me think it over?"

I decided midway during our conversation that I could not mention what I had done. I had to be man enough to bear the consequence face to face. Krish was going through a lot, even if he did not show it. He was successful at compartmentalizing his emotions. A byproduct he had once said, acquired through years of dealing in logic trees and flowgraphs. In coping with the loss of his father, he had already created a compartment. I guessed it wouldn't lead to a stack overflow if another variable filled that container. "Emotions are like a virus, a common cold, disrupting the flow of logic in people's minds," is what I remember him lecturing me about during a debate we once had on AI.

I on the other hand, had not been successfully neutered in that department.

I called Kelly. "Can you talk?"

"Sure. What's on your mind?"

I told Kelly what had happened, the shootout, my injury and how I lost Maya. She listened to me, not saying a word. An occasional gasp was all that came over the phone.

At the end she spoke: "Dan, I had no idea. Is there anything you need?"

"I'll be fine, thanks. I'd like to move forward. I'm done with grieving."

"I understand," she said.

"Would you like to start work on the ideas we had, or are you in the middle of something?" I said.

"I'm ready when you are," she said.

"Maya's brother, Krish… I've invited him to stay with me for a while. Can we meet when he's here? I'd like him to be involved."

"You take the lead on this, Dan. I trust you."

"OK, let me convince him to come."

"Dan… if there's anything at all, pick the phone."

"I will." I said. "I see work as a vaccine to preempt any bout of depression."

Maya had walked to the kitchen. I noticed her dismembered torso when she moved behind the kitchen counter. The random path algorithm of the apartment navigation was working; only my Maya would not ever be able to bite into those apples she kept on the counter-top. There were two apples still in the bowl. I couldn't hold back the tear that escaped. I looked through the blurry streak it left on the Wizer. Maybe I had not thought everything through. There was a reason people only kept a photograph as a reminder of times gone by. Was it mockery? I was too confused to think straight anymore. I needed help, and I could not discount that it might be of the professional kind.

The prime requisite to execute Kelly's project would be clarity of thought and general sanity. Therefore I had to know if I was going mad, and if not, then I could use Krish's help on the project. He could also get his mind off things. It was only after much deliberation that I picked up the phone yet again in the afternoon and called him. I remembered him telling me he would think about coming. I was impatient.

...

Krish answered on the first ring.

"Hi, is everything alright?"

"Actually, it's not," I said. "There's something I have to tell... show you."

"What is it?" he said. I could hear the worry in his voice.

"It wouldn't be fair to have you come here and then show you what I have to."

"What are you talking about?"

"Give me a second. Switch to video call."

He accepted. I put the phone on speaker and placed it on the table.

"Where are you? I see the apartment. Flip the camera."

"You're seeing the view from the Wizer," I said. I slowly turned.

"What the fuck are you doing?" Krish's voice rose. "Dan, what the fuck… talk to me."

"I don't know myself. I may be going mad. I don't know. I miss her so much." I felt my eyes brimming.

"Turn it off Dan, turn the damn machine off."

I removed the Wizer.

After the silence that followed, it was him who spoke first. "Why would you do that? You have to let her go." His voice was faltering.

"I don't want to. I can't. You would not understand. I don't know if I do. I didn't even get to say bye to her. Like a fucking idiot, the only time I could tell her I loved her was when she would never hear me." I was half crying, half talking.

He listened in silence. I could only hear him draw in his breath through his mouth repeatedly.

"Listen to me," he said. "I didn't know both of you were having a relationship. I chalked it up to harmless flirting. In hindsight I can understand why you may have wanted to keep it secret. But that's all in the past now. I miss her too," he continued, "more than I can show, but I wouldn't want that kind of torture by having her ghost walk around. You have to let her go, Dan."

"She's not a ghost," I said.

I picked up the phone and switched on its front camera. Both our faces were flushed and our eyes red. I grabbed the remote and turned on the projector.

"What are you doing?" he demanded.

"Take a look," I said, turning the phone around to show him the projection screen. "Why is it OK to sit all day in front of a life-sized slide show and remember the good times?" I switched the Wizer back on. "Yet it's abnormal to want to see the person you love right beside you?"

Maya was sitting on the couch with her headset on, eyes closed, and barely bobbing her head to the music. I looked down at my phone screen through the Wizer. Krish was watching, tears flowing, forming two streams down to the sides of his mouth. He covered his mouth and nose with his hands.

"Look at her," I said. "I don't want her to be a just a memory. I want to keep her memory alive. That day, the Wizer was part of the reason for three deaths. Today, it's keeping me from dying inside."

"Help me, Krish," I said. "Help me keep her memory alive." He was listening. He wiped his eyes with his hands. I took the Wizer off. "Put it back on," he said.

I replaced the Wizer and we sat looking at Maya. She still had her eyes closed. Then she got up from the couch and walked toward the window.

"What's she doing?" he asked.

"It must be 5:00 p.m.," I said. "The first thing she would do when she came here after dance practice was to stand by the window and chide me for not opening the curtains. She always said how beautiful the sky looked in the evenings and at sunrise." I limped as fast as I could to the window and flung open the curtains. Back on the couch Krish and I watched through the Wizer as she stood by the window gazing out.

"That's part of the routine I put into the apartment frame," I said.

"When do you want me to come there?"

"On the next flight," I said.

...

It was four days later that I was at the airport waiting for Krish's plane to land. I could walk short distances, but used a cane for support. The doctor said that I would be good as new soon, provided I didn't overexert. I heard him, but I wasn't going to let Krish take a taxi. He walked out of immigration, smiling as he spotted me. We hugged each other like brothers reunited after a tour of duty. On the way home he remarked how he missed the city.

"Move back here then," I said.

"Not so easy to just move. Besides, it's best for Mom there. At least she has a support system," he said, "and who knows? Maybe you'll be the one moving there.

AYREE still needs us."

"How long do you think before the project is resurrected?" I asked.

"It was never on hold. You can't keep the military on hold. The Prof. is in touch with me," he said. "They are keeping it low profile. The proposal is that AYREE has exclusive rights to usage of the IP we contributed for products or systems destined for any military and homeland security use, and we are free to license the usage to other markets.

"They are willing to give us a onetime payment for an exclusive license for that usage. What do you think?"

"It sounds good to me," I said. "It would have just been ideas, if we did not have access to their resources. We already have a client for the entertainment market," I said.

"Who?"

"Do you remember Kelly? The call that came in? Her father is a media tycoon." I pulled into the gas station a few miles outside the airport to tank up.

"I miss the peri-peri cheese sticks from in there," he said, pointing to the 24-7.

"Let's get some," I said, "but first get your cell-phone out and connect to the wifi hotspot."

Krish connected to the station's wifi. The welcome page said: Digital Fuel. He clicked it, and his phone's camera turned on. He located the augmented digital fuel pump overlaid besides the real fuel pump.

"Your idea?" he asked.

"Yeah. Trial run for Kelly's dad. He has a soda company

as the client sponsoring it."

"All these tunes are free?" asked Krish as he scrolled a playlist of down-loadable songs from the fuel station.

"Yeah, sponsored," I said. "The idea is to tank up on digital juice while you wait."

We reached home, and Krish went out to the sundeck. The city lights twinkled below.

"I missed this view," he said.

I pointed to the dusty lounger. "I never told you this before, but I used to get such grief from Maya if it was left dusty. It was her favorite spot."

He managed a smile and shifted his gaze lower.

"Where is she?" he asked.

"Inside."

We went back inside, and he connected his Wizer to the home network. We sat on the floor and looked at Maya on the couch. She was asleep.

"What time does she sleep?" he asked.

"Eleven p.m. She always claimed she was a morning person," I said. "So I filled the frame with that data for time of day activity."

He smiled and ran a finger across his eyes.

"Why?" I asked.

"She used to go upstairs to her room at ten," he said. "Now we know it was to spend an hour with you."

"Is this wrong Krish? I need to know."

"I can't answer you. I have different beliefs." He took off the Wizer, his hand making a fist around it.

"Different beliefs? You can't put the Wizer down can you? You hesitate even now." I took it from his hand. "Don't you feel good when you remember something from back in your childhood?"

He looked at me a little confused. "I suppose."

"Now tell me in how much detail you remember that childhood memory?" I didn't wait for him to answer. "Chances are it's gradually getting muddy. It's fading. Those memories are slowly dying out." He stared at the floor. He may have been trying to pull up a long forgotten memory.

"Well, I refuse to let Maya be only a memory to me. She used to always ask, "In which parallel universe are you living, Dan?" I guess I can answer her now. "You know what the best part about Maya being reborn is Krish?" He looked at me. "That there is hope that she may create memories with me." There was a look of utter shock on his face.

"I don't know if that's possible, but unlike the current world in which a person is taken away, the way she was, for no logical reason… I choose to challenge that construct and at some point hope to let the one who I love; live. I'll find a way to do it."

He listened in silence. After a long while he spoke, "You know you're treading dangerous ground here. We've chosen not to focus too much on these issues in AI, although I'll tell you, we are curious." He went on. "You realize that there is no free-will in something that we create with AI. Everything functions within rules and parameters."

"Free will, Krish? You think we function with free will?

We have rules and constraints... it's called religion. If you fight or question those constraints, I suppose you get pulled out of the game by some providential referee."

He may have touched a nerve in me, a nerve that I was trying my best to suppress ever since Maya was taken away for no fault of hers.

"Heck, sometimes you get pulled out for no logical reason. Maybe it's a sacred random subroutine being run once in a while, huh Krish? You tell me. You're the AI expert." My mouth felt parched. "If we truly had free will, then we should have been given the ability to change or at least be able to choose how that routine gets executed–that terminal routine."

"And it is what you intend to do?" he asked. "Listen to you!"

"No, I'm only attempting to bend the rules. Maybe someday if the rules bend enough, they break. Then we can start to address free will. She does not have free will, I accept that," I said, handing him the Wizer. "She can walk only within the confines of this room, and she dies if the plug is pulled. But in a way, it is not that different from our so-called free will is it?"

All the while we were arguing, Maya was asleep. She was only executing explicit code after all.

"You once said that we are all creatures of habit, didn't you?" I asked.

He looked at me, nodding in affirmation.

"Will you help me modify the frame's database, so we

can add to it, one habit at a time? I want to add our memories together, one at a time."

He must have heard the plea in my voice. "Let's take a look at everything first thing in the morning?"

...

We slept in the bedroom, Krish on the bed, and I took a mattress on the floor. When I awoke, it was to the sound of music coming from the living room I looked at my phone. It was 11:00 a.m. I used the bed as support to stand and went outside. He was seated on the floor with the Wizer on and his laptop opened, gazing at the window near the scope.

"Maya's there?" I asked.

He nodded and gave me the Wizer. She was such a pretty sight. I'd never seen her dance before. I knew she was good, but she never did a full dance from start to finish for me; a pirouette or a classical pose was all I would get.

"The scope's in the way," I said, walking to move it.

"No don't!"

I stopped.

"Don't move it. I'm working on a proximity trigger occlusion mask."

I gave him his Wizer and put mine on. Maya gracefully avoided the telescope and danced around it, never cutting through it.

"Don't you need some kind of AI to drive and modify the performance capture file to do that?" I asked.

“I had recorded Maya's performance a while ago. It was supposed to be a present for her.”

“What do you mean?”

“I was supposed to have programmed it to show her any imperfect moves and stress loads around her ankle, by superimposing her live mocap session from a FishEye over these perfected moves,” he said. “I never completed the project.”

“She's moving just perfect to me. She had given up asking me to come to her recitals. I never knew she was this good.”

“I've adapted her mocap file using human IK rules and procedural adaptation of the motion.”

“Whoa! You lost me.”

“What that means is, she can walk around the apartment and interact naturally with obstacles. I've patched in routines AYREE had developed for an articulated droi...d.” He trailed off and looked away. I walked over and put my hand on his shoulder. He sighed. “The AI system is now connected to the FishEye up there,” he pointed to the wall. “Using the apartment frame, I've populated it with objects in your apartment. Not everything, but we can add entities as we go along.” Krish opened what looked like a huge scrolling spreadsheet. “Take that bar stool for instance,” he pointed to it at the far end of the kitchen. “The FishEye has run an edge detect and stereo match on it, and it's feeding it to the main AI driving...”

“Maya.” I completed his sentence. “It's OK Krish, I know how you must feel.”

He only looked down at his laptop. “These AI algorithms were written for a mechanical drone. It was never meant for a Digital Surrogate.”

“That's exactly who Maya is! I refuse to think of her as gone,” I said, easing myself onto the floor. “She's just in another place, and we're interacting with her Dirrogate. Just as you were interacting with mine at the DRONE lab.”

A strange weight was lifted off us with that revelation. Granted, a digital surrogate had a human operator. Given time, I was sure that Krish's expertise in algorithms would probably surpass the intellect of the many human operators who might want to buy a Wizer and own a Dirrogate.

I said. “If I move the stool near where she is now?–”

“Will she sit on it? No,” he said. “I mean, she doesn't have to. The AI knows it's a bar-stool and will run the human IK accordingly, which will transpose her to sit on the stool in much the same way you did the sit motion for the couch.” He lifted the Wizer, squeezed his eyes shut and pinched the bridge of his nose between his thumb and forefinger. “But she doesn't have to sit. She can choose to navigate around it.”

“Choice?” I asked.

“It's not free will, but yes it's choice, for lack of a better definition,” he said.

I wore the Wizer and watched in disbelief as Maya came near us, paused, looked at Krish and I on the floor, then smiled and turned to sit on the couch in her favorite pose. He pointed to the FishEye on the wall and said, “Live depth map stream of the room. Your face and voice signature, identifies you."

"Can Satish create a better model of Maya's face?" I asked.

"I have 3D meshes from her performance capture," he said, "so technically, yes. But hi-rez photo scans of her I don't. Besides it's going to raise a lot of questions and eyebrows there," he said.

"We'll have to devise some excuse for that," I said. "Tell him it's a video of one of Maya's dance performances for your mother."

"It could work. The model would have to be realistic enough to pass off as video. We still have the question of getting hi-rez scans."

We looked at each other, perhaps realizing that we knew the next question. It was Krish who vocalized it.

"Do you know any of her passwords?"

"No," I said.

"Neither do I," he said. "If we could access her cloud storage, there could be some portfolio pictures."

"Try a brute force password guess?"

We updated the dictionary to take into account different combinations of phrases and words that Maya might have used and let the password cracker do its job overnight.

...

In the morning, I was up at the same time as him. We went

to his laptop. The dictionary attack was not successful at coming up with a possible password.

"Maybe her PC at home has an automated login to some sites," he said, "But I won't know until I get back."

Then I remembered.

"Hang on. I have a video of Maya from the day she was at my place when you called..." My voice trailed off as I remembered she was not wearing much in the video. I scrolled through the media on my phone and found it.

"Let me check it and see," I said to Krish and walked away. He understood. I played back the video and saw her typing when I had zoomed in on her, but there was no clear view of the keyboard. "It's no use. She's typing but the keys are not visible," I said.

"But she's typing?" he said. "Acoustic cryptanalysis is worth a try."

I'd only heard of that term in passing on hacking forums. I found it too far-fetched to be practical.

"Extract the audio track and give it to me. I understand you'd rather give just the audio."

I nodded. I exported the audio from the time I had started recording till she said, "Changing my social status." He loaded it into his laptop. I peered over his shoulder and then saw that the software he had on was real. It even had a GUI with the AYREE logo on it. He looked at me and then walked to my laptop. "Keep quiet," he said, as he pressed every key on it.

I understood what he was doing. Each key made a distinct sound when pressed. He was going to match it in his analysis software. While the program was doing the analysis, I asked, "What exactly do you do at AYREE?"

"Don't worry. I'm legit," he managed a smile. "It's a hobby and curiosity. I got the package on my laptop only because I have clearance from DRONE."

We had an answer.

At least the login to her social profile. It was a pseudo portmanteau of our names. I put on my Wizer and went up close, reaching out to her. She backed up a step and smiled.

"4ever," I said, repeating the end phrase of her password. Krish was watching me. He logged into the website. In one of the system mails was her account details to her cloud hard-drive. In it were all the photographs we needed. They were from a professional portfolio shoot. There was a folder of photos labeled "Sunrise" that had about 300 pictures of day-breaks dating back a few years.

"Could we write a macro," I said, "that allows Maya to log in and re-post one of these pictures at random?"

He thought about what I was asking, took a moment and then said, "It's not a problem to implement. But did you think of the consequences?"

"What do you mean?"

"Her network of friends will get updates," he said.

"Caption the pictures as posted by me."

The next morning I woke to a status update of a new picture posted by Maya. I was tagged in it. Below the picture it read: "It's a new day. Let's make new memories. Posted by

@Dan, for Maya." Krish had given the AI, access to Maya's social network via my laptop.

CHAPTER SEVEN

WE WERE ON OUR WAY to meet Kelly and her Dad. I managed to clean up and wore a blazer, in case first impressions mattered to him. Traffic was light and the weather pleasant enough to drive with the top down. Krish used his Wizer as sunglasses. He held his face against the wind and was breathing deeply.

"All this pure oxygen is going to ruin me," he said.

"I kinda miss the diesel fumes outside AYREE," I joked.

"Something was disturbing me about that evening in the club." Krish said.

"What do mean?" I looked at him quizically.

"I went through the log data of the Wizer you wore. I saw you shake your head that one time."

"Yeah, so did that guy. I'd disengaged his head as the target node and selected his shoulder."

"Exactly. The algorithm should not have locked onto the head as first choice. The head node even had a higher risk factor for movement."

"I would have killed him. I didn't want that."

"The AI was simply executing the most effective means of neutralizing a threat – Extermination."

"Is it programmed that way?" I asked

"No... that is the point. The algorithm grows by learning it's wearer's habits, remember?"

"Hang on a sec, what are you getting at? I'm not infecting your AI, OK."

"I'm not saying you're a virus. I'm not saying you might have a psychotic thread running in you..." Krish smiled and then probably realized the inappropriateness of it.

"Yeah," I said. "I disengaged that node."

"As you should. But there are serious ethical issues I have to look into with this code. It's evolving, but might be picking up human...traits; buried deep in our DNA."

"The last thing we need is AI DNA getting infected with human carcinogens - hatred, greed...that kind of shit," I said.

The GPS on the dashboard beeped. We were nearing

Henry Tan's building. "What kind of deal you think we should look for?" Krish asked.

"Let's play it by ear." I said. "If we get along with him, money will follow. We'll see what he's like for now."

He nodded without looking at me. We parked outside the imposing glass and steel building that looked at least 15 floors high. In bold red were the letters TAN. No Tan Industries, or Tan Media. Simply, TAN. I liked that. The woman at the reception desk looked up our names.

"Yes. Mr. Tan is expecting you. Daniel, Krish."

We took our visitor badges.

"Press the red button with the T," she said.

When we got out of the elevator, Kelly was holding the door to the meeting room open. She left it and came running. She almost knocked me off balance when she hugged me.

"Missed you." She kissed me on the cheek.

"Same here," I said. "Go easy. My leg's just about healing."

"Oh! I'm sorry," she said. She took my backpack off my shoulder.

"I'm Kelly. You must be Krish?" She smiled.

"Kelly, Krish… vice versa," I said.

"Nice to meet you," he said.

He couldn't shake her hand because his were occupied balancing a box that had the Quad in it and his computer on top.

"Dad will be here soon. Would you like coffee?"

"That would be great. Thanks," I said.

We busied ourselves setting up the Quad. Krish jumped up on the conference table much to our surprise. He had to attach the FishEye on the huge TV on the wall. We stood when Mr. Tan walked in about ten minutes later.

"Hi, Daniel... and you must be Krish?" He offered his hand.

I shook it. "Mr. Tan."

"Please, call me Henry. My associates do, and I have a good feeling about you," he said.

"Thank you, Henry."

"Good of you to come, Krish. Kelly mentioned you and Daniel are working on some outstanding technology."

"Thank you, and it's nice to be here, Mr. Tan," Krish said.

"It's Henry to you too," he said with a wide grin.

"Daniel, I'm getting good feedback on the digital fuel campaign. No sense in wasting time. Let's roll with it ASAP," he said. "How would you like to do this? One off payment, license, or partnership?"

At that moment I decided I liked Mr. Henry Tan. "I didn't put much thought into it. Can I get back with an answer on that tomorrow?"

"Sure! Take two days. But let's get an answer, so we can get cracking."

He had a no-nonsense, straight talking style. His eyes only showed the slightest crow's feet when he smiled. He didn't look old enough to be Kelly's father, more an elder brother. Kelly must get her anime-girl eyes from her mother.

"Any new ideas?" Henry probed.

"Yes." I walked to a table at the side and poured two glasses of water. I placed them on the Quad which was sitting on the floor. Krish started the app on his phone, and the Quad rose a few feet and flew to the center of the conference table. I held my hand out and it paused, backtracked and floated over without spilling a drop. It reached its destination, Henry's chair. The Quad hovered in front of him, while he took the glass.

"It knows its destination," Krish said.

"In reality it will be much easier," I said, "with a defined flight path from bar to customer's table."

"Now this we need," Henry said, applauding.

"I'm sure bar orders will increase with the cool factor alone," said Kelly.

"Yes. But efficiency of service on crowded nights is the big selling point in my book," Henry said.

We saved the Wizer for last. Krish went through all the possible scenarios and explained why we believed the Wizer would be a must-have device in every home. From first aid augmentation, to social applications, to sport and tourism; Krish put it through it's paces. Kelly and I watched as Henry paid keen attention, asking questions and at times, taking notes. He got technology. He was a futurist. I liked him. I envied him, because he looked healthy, stress-free and could carry off a business suit.

There were things about the Wizer we did not tell Henry

Tan that morning. We did not tell him we believed it would be an essential part of every person's life. We did not tell him that when social network updates from loved ones ceased, or on nights when nightlife and music weren't going to cut it and there was only hurt and pain; people could sit at home with their Wizers on and create new memories *with* their cherished ones who had since transcended the human life cycle. That might be too much to handle, even for a futurist of Mr. Tan's caliber.

It was midday, and the temperature had climbed a bit. We got back to the car, but I kept the top down. There was a lot to discuss on how best to approach a deal with Henry Tan. Krish agreed that he was a likable and straight businessman. We felt that a proposal to begin and run an offshoot of TAN would be a great start.

Krish mentioned that while he was proud of his AI work, competition would soon catch up and swallow us whole once our ideas showed business potential. For that reason alone we needed a sharp businessman with a commercial umbrella above us. I agreed that it would take the edge off and allow us to concentrate on what we did best: create.

"What about our deal with AYREE?" I said, "What options do you think we have for IP ownership?"

He was about to answer when his phone rang.

"Hello Professor," Krish said and looked at me. "OK... fine. No, professor, I'll be there."

After his call ended I asked. "When?"

"Tomorrow. I'll check if there's an earlier flight," he said.

"What's on the cards?"

"The Prof. told me DRONE is back on track. We need to talk and sort out roles and negotiate a deal," Krish said. "Would you like to join me?"

"No, you go," I said. "I just got back. Besides you can handle them, and I'll follow up with Henry."

"Makes sense." He turned to look at the tiny rear seat and then back at me. "I miss her."

"Me too," I said. "The lowest point in my life was paying off my bills with Singh's dirty money."

"Given a choice, even I'd like to take our work out of there. But we're under contract," said Krish. "Much worse, they already have all the code."

"Better us, than another Singh nurturing those algorithms." I nodded, agreeing. "Logic over Emotion...right?"

...

We got home, and put our Wizers on. It was the most natural thing in the world to do. Maya was near the PC. She was scanning news feeds of the topics that interested her and clipping out headlines. Krish had noticed she would collect articles on classical dance and nature photography. The AI was scraping the same sites she used to–clipping pictures and articles and time stamping them. Krish walked over to the laptop on a corner table. I followed, peering over his shoulder. Reams of words and numbers scrolled by. Krish tabbed to a spreadsheet like screen with rows and columns.

"The Frame?" I asked.

"Yes. The algorithms are at work, mining data from her social feed over the past few years. Digital bread crumbs she unknowingly left behind..."

I looked at Krish and then back at the screen, watching social networing website screens rapidly flash in and out of view.

"Making sense of all this data will take a while, even though I'm offloading the heavy lifting to AYREE's mainframes," he said.

"I think you should take the hi-rez face images with you, instead of sending them to Satish," I said.

"Yes, it's better if I'm there with him while he's working on them."

The taxi to take Krish to the airport was waiting at the building at 11:00 p.m. He managed to get a late night flight that had seats empty. We said our goodbyes, but I knew he would have to come back again. We would certainly have a launch event once things were signed up with Henry.

I closed the door and lay on the carpet near where Maya slept on the couch. When I used to sleep there I remembered her coming and lightly kissing my forehead and covering me with a quilt. I wished I could do the same for her. I put on the projector and pulled up our pictures. It was not the same. There was no comparison between seeing her picture on the screen and the experience of seeing Maya through the Wizer sleeping on the couch. She was in the room with me; It was a parallel universe, and I was grateful we could bridge it.

Krish was on video call with me from AYREE. He sounded upbeat. "They're willing to pay us quite a bit," he said, "as well as offer stock options in AYREE to keep us interested in working with them in military and homeland security."

"Define quite a bit?" I said, smiling.

"Three point two million each," he continued, "to sign over IP and guarantee continuity of work with them for two years."

"What do you think?"

"Should I even answer?" I smiled. It was infectious.

"Here's the good part. We build a secure network for you to visit," he said. "You can work via Dirrogate."

"You're kidding me!"

"I knew it would stall discussions if I asked you to move here. So from the start I told Prof. Kumar this is how it would work best."

"He agreed without a fight?" I said.

"Yeah, he saw opportunity in the proposal."

"How so?"

"He said if we don't hit any glitches in interaction between a human and a Dirrogate, then we have something else to patent."

"Importing Dirrogate talent?" I laughed.

"We don't import talent here. We export it," Krish said. "And if there's a business model in there, why not!"

I remembered the last time we were happy. It turned out to be short lived. It may have been because of my confusion as to who I had to be thankful to for my good fortune. This time I was in control. I wasn't going to attribute my feeling of euphoria to the whim of some super-being. This time, I would own my happiness. James' immortal words came to mind: "Happiness, you my bitch."

"What's the next step?" I asked.

"Let's wait for them to draw up paperwork, and we'll go over it for loopholes," he said. "If all looks good to you, we sign up and start work?"

"What about Singh? A verdict?" I asked.

"Hello, Daniel. Let me answer you?" Prof. Kumar had walked in through the door behind Krish.

"Hello, Professor Kumar."

"Daniel, I haven't spoken with you since..." said the Prof. "My deepest regret for everything leading to the loss of our beloved Maya." He placed his hand on Krish's shoulder.

"Thank you, Prof." I said. "What happens to Mr. Singh?"

"There's to be more hearings. In India, these things can take years. But he's off the board. It was a unanimous vote against him. I hope he regrets what he made happen as much as I do."

"How did this terror cell manage to infiltrate a high profile institution like AYREE?" I asked.

"The weakest link in the chain, Daniel," said the Prof, "was greed. Unfortunately Mr. Singh was the proxy.

"You see, we are a honey-pot to organizations seeking world disorder."

"I don't understand," I said. "You are not an exporter of terror."

"Precisely. We are not on the international sanctions radar or labeled as terror exporters," said the Prof. "In fact we never belonged there. That is the reason, we are fertile grounds for these terror organizations. They come to shop here." The Prof. pulled up a chair and leaned in closer. "We are not on any red alert list. So intelligence, software and hardware are available here. Unfortunately, even high caliber intellect is for sale."

"I see. I get your point," I said.

"What we have not rid ourselves of is corruption and greed," he said.

"And that is our shortcoming–"

"Which these terror organizations capitalize on." I finished for him.

"AYREE's main goals are AI development for the military, homeland security and also other fields. Augmented reality and AI go hand in hand," said the Prof. "This is my belief and is why I am keen for you and Krish to continue with us."

"The Wizer, as you named it, changed our course of research on the DRONE project. We won't be researching AI for robot drones in the short term," he said. "The Quad and a human partner will be the new drone team." The Prof. stood and aligned his chair. "Not putting the human member of the team in harm's way is our priority," he was quick to clarify.

"I'm happy to be on board, Professor," I said. "The Wizer has changed the course of my life too."

Krish turned to look at the phone screen.

"I'll leave you to talk with Krish," he said, "and welcome back onboard, Daniel."

"Thank you, Professor."

"I've given the photos to Satish," Krish said, after the Prof. left the room.

"What's his take on it?"

"He wasn't nosy. He's only glad to help. I told him it's a family thing I want done for Mom."

"Is she back home?" I asked.

"No, she wants to stay there longer. As long as she's happy, I'm fine with it."

"That's good. She has gone through much in this year," I said.

"I'm going to drop in on Satish. Call you later?"

...

"Put on your Wizer. We're going cruising," Krish said when he called two days later. He had been working overtime with Satish. He claimed to have slept for not more than four hours in total, yet he sounded more excited than I'd ever heard him before.

"Has Satish completed it?" I asked.

"He's still working on perfecting every aspect. He's dropped everything else for this."

"OK, where are we going?"

"Co-ords are 18°57'N 72°48'E."

"Waiting on connect," I said.

I had the Wizer on and was sitting on my couch.

"Yeah, it's uploading new graphics and user interface routines to you," he said.

I was looking out of the window. The evening sun had made an appearance. Maya was going through one of her classical dance routines. I noticed the way she closed her eyes when she twirled and then opened them ever so slowly when the move was completed.

"Woah! What was that?" The initialization of the new upgrade caught me by surprise.

All of a sudden the live view coming through the Wizer disintegrated into a thousand squares and flew down a worm hole. My gaze followed one of the video chips that had a piece of the scope and the curtains mapped to it. It twisted, spiraling its way down the hole. The imagery was replaced by a street I recognized immediately as Mumbai. I was in the middle of the road and on instinct, ducked as a car came right at me.

"Stand," he shouted, "and walk to the pavement."

I stood up from the couch and walked three steps to my right. When I turned, Krish came into view. Only he looked very real. I understood what was happening. His Dirrogate was mapped with live video in-situ. He wore his Wizer and his eyes were visible through the tint of the polarizers.

"Care to enlighten me more?" I asked. I couldn't help turning around and seeing so many people walking past me, It was almost claustrophobic. Over the sound of horns and street children playing, he explained. "I was with Satish and he had these ideas for enhancing the Wizer's visuals. You know how the environment artists are," he said.

"Not artists; CGI demigods," I corrected him.

"He said perception is in the eye of the beholder… or something to that effect."

"Maybe he said realism?" I offered.

"Yeah. Maybe. Turns out he is a believer and subscribes to the concept of transhumanism," Krish said, adjusting the Wizer on the bridge of his nose. "He believes the catalyst for widespread acceptance of our evolution as digital beings has to be based on visual fidelity, or the entire construct will be stymied by the human brain and mind."

"Hmm… the uncanny valley effect? It has to be love at first sight, huh?"

"Didn't know you followed the movement," he said.

"We are evolving, Krish. Look around us. Am I really with you in person?"

"Point taken," he said. "So… Satish showed me a demo of the Quad acquiring real-time depth and texture maps."

"Nothing new in that," I said.

"Yeah, but look above us."

I tilted my head up. The crude shape of the Quad came into view.

"The Quad is here, but you can't see it because the Fish-Eye is on it aimed straight ahead."

"So it's mapping video texture over the live geometry. Cool," I said.

"Yeah, the breakthrough is I can freeze a frame... freeze real life as it were, step out of the scene and study it."

"All you do is block out the live world with the cross polarizers?"

"Yeah," he said. "It's a big deal for AYREE to be able to use such data-sets."

"The resolution has improved," I said.

"Good observation," he said. "So has the range sensing. The lens optics have also been upgraded."

"I noticed that if I turn around I don't see the live feed, just the empty street," I said.

"Yes, of course," he replied. "The Quad is facing the other way around. It's why I'm standing in front of you. The whole street, however, is a 3D model done by a standard laser scan taken from the top of that high tower." Krish pointed to a building block at the far end of the street. I turned back to the live 3D view again. He walked in front of me.

"This is uber cool. Everyone looks so real."

"You should see how cool it is when you're here in person with the Wizer on," he said. "I'm here watching these real people pass by, only they have a mesh of themselves mapped onto them."

"Ahhh! Yes."

"Yeah, it's like they have living paint on them. I feel like reaching out and touching, just to feel the texture."

"I'm sure you do! Especially her texture."

A girl in jeans and heels approached. She had a perfect

catwalk gait. She smiled at Krish and walked on.

“Did you see that? She looked right through me,” I said.

“Yeah spooky right? How's she to know you're here?”

We laughed.

“She must think you're nuts, talking to yourself,” I said.

“I thought about that, so I've got my wired headset connected.” He dangled the wire in front of me.

“Everything you see is a 3D model being rendered live. With such huge data-sets being recorded and compressed, we can travel back in time, so to speak... A *Parallel World,*” he said.

We walked forward, not realizing that I was actually teletraveling. “I'm going to bump into my wall.” I said.

“Use the GUI to move forward. I'll send the Quad with you and catch up.”

I stood still in my room and used the touch screen to navigate forward. My Dirrogate took a few steps, and the Quad appeared above me.

“Wait up,” he said. He turned and sat on a bench on the pavement. I caught up with him.

“The Prof. told me some disturbing news. It involved us, and some of Mr. Singh's friends,” said Krish. We were in a quieter corner of the street.

“East European friends?”

“Yes. It seems we, you and I, were head hunted by Mr. Singh,” said Krish. “You were right when you said that they found me. I'd sent feelers about my work in AI to institutions in India.” He hesitated then asked, “Is that the only reason you came? You were running away?"

"I'm sorry, Krish. I took credit for coming when I should have told you the real reason. I was desperate in more ways than one."

"Singh knows how to hire. He investigates backgrounds, finds weaknesses. He knew my need for money; Dad's treatment. He feeds off people's desperation; buys loyalty."

"This is beginning to make sense now," I said. "The visit from Cheryl and Magnus. They work for him?"

"Yes. They're not head hunters. Scoping us was a favor they did for him. They were interested in selling A.I.R.I AI code and solutions that Singh siphoned out." Krish stood up. "Their latest interest was in selling compromised versions of the Wizer-Mesh Arm Cast on the black market."

"Compromised... leaving a back door open?" I said.

"There is a big demand for such kind of weaponry where a central authority can control Mercenaries, police forces... terrorists," said Krish walking to the edge of the footpath and gesturing to the crowds walking. "A public rally can go horribly wrong, if a single riot police officer can be remote controlled, to maim - or kill."

"Fuck! a Human Drone," I said. He nodded.

"My algorithms need a code of Ethics."

It was late evening, and the sun had almost set.

"I have something to show you." Krish's tone was different. I waited for him to overtake me, then I took a few steps back. Even the video mapped version of him, couldn't disguise his nervousness.

He crossed his fingers, cracking his knuckles.

"Krish, all OK?"

"Punch in these co-ords," he said.

"You'll arrive before me, so wait there. It's nearby, but I'll have to reach you by bike."

"Tele-traveling...now," I said.

I punched in the new co-ords and again the same funky warp travel sequence activated. The street we were on disintegrated and got sucked into the wormhole. I found myself on the terrace of a house. It was Krish's place. The pool was familiar, so was his deck chair and the kitchen door that Maya poked her head from the first time we connected. It was all such a long time ago. Looking around, I spotted the FishEye up on a corner wall. That was where the live texture feed was coming from. Krish entered from the kitchen door and walked toward me.

"Thanks for coming," he said.

"It's beautiful," I said, looking at fluffy white clouds slowly taking on an orange hue. A few kites floated in the distance perhaps hunting before darkness fell.

"This is not what I wanted to show you," he said. "Look towards the recliner in the corner." I turned in the direction he was pointing. A gray haired man emerged, passing right through the closed door. He walked to the chair. In his hand he had a newspaper. He gracefully sat in the chair, lifted the newspaper and looked down at it.

"Your Daa–" My mouth hung open on the word.

"Yes," he said and started walking toward the chair. I

used the touchscreen and followed him. The skin on his father's face looked so real I almost reached out to touch it, knowing full well there would be no tactile response.

"How… why…" I didn't know to form the question, much less complete it.

"After I saw Maya, I had to," he said. "I've used her same frame structure for the newspaper reading. Last night I went through old photos, his things, his books," his voice was low. "I'm feeding them into the frame. This was his life for the past two years before the cancer claimed him. Every evening he would sit in this chair in the old house and read his paper."

I listened in silence as he spoke. Tactile receptors weren't needed to experience pain. Tone of voice transported those spores just as easily.

"It was easy to create a frame for him, Dan," he said. "In the time that the cancer was eating away at him, the day's routine became more predictable. At first he would still go to work, then come home and spend time with us. Then he couldn't go anymore and he was at home all day. I knew his routine so well it took me less than a day feed it in. There was no need for any random branches."

I turned to look at him. The Wizer hid his eyes well. "Krish," I said. "You know what the best part about having him back is? It does not have to be the way it was. You can re-define his routine. Ask your mom what made your dad happy and feed that in. Build on old memories, build new ones and feed those in. You're the AI designer… bend the rules."

"I dare not show her anything like this," he said. "She would never understand. There's something not right about resurrecting the dead. There's a reason why people say rest in peace."

"Every time you think of your dad, and Maya, you're resurrecting them. Why shouldn't they continue to live in this world while they rest in the other? It was not as though they went there by their own will. They were taken away from us." I relaxed my grip on my phone after I heard the crunch of plastic. "We're claiming them back."

"So you're a God now? Is that what it is?"

"No, but somewhere out there, a higher form of sadism - has won the first round. Well, fuck that...I'm not ready to be *pwned*."

There was a long silence. The only sounds were of our breathing and crickets on his terrace. I sat on the floor in my apartment. Krish sat on the concrete floor next to his dad. There was no distance anymore. I was convinced what we were doing might not be so wrong. I lifted my phone. He looked at it.

"Where are you going?" he asked.

"Nowhere. I'm calling Maya."

Within seconds Maya tele-traveled to the terrace. She turns around slow; a whole circle, then walked to the chair her father was sitting on."

"It's strange to see the algorithms evolving this way..."

"I don't see it the way you do," I said. "I see it as Maya recognizing her father."

Krish moved closer to me. “I need a picture of them, together,” he said. Maya's hands came up to her Father's head. She bent and kissed the back of his head. He did not react.

“No, Krish... we're not playing God. We're only attempting to set things right,” I said.

CHAPTER EIGHT

THE HARD-DRIVE IN MY laptop always made a click-whirring sound when it was accessed. Of the two drives, the one with the operating system had the problem. Every time it whirred, I would mumble,"Please, please, please," as if by the power of suggestion the head would skip the bad sector and not ask for a re-start.

I woke up to that sound and grabbed my Wizer from the floor where I had fallen asleep. The curtains were open. Sure enough, Maya was at the laptop. It was just before 6 am, and one of those mornings when Maya was uploading a sunrise photo. She looked different. She was the same Maya as I remembered on that footbridge–the same Maya on that terrace, looking down at me while the sun caught the highlights in her hair. I walked closer, and she smiled. If she could speak, what would she say?

The only other person with access to my network was Krish. He must have worked all night. The litmus test was what I had witnessed in his home. With him creating a Dirrogate of his father, if I knew him well, he would not stop. The next node in a logic flow graph for him would be AI integration.

Even that Maya's hair had highlights and there was subsurface scattering on her skin, needed some kind of AI working in the background. I understood the logic behind how it was done. He had probably used the co-ordinates of where Maya was to sync with the sun's location. With the FishEye on my wall, the indoor light sources were being matched and rendered. What else might he do to bridge our worlds–was the question.

...

It had been a month of hard work, but I made time to visit Mom and Dad and take them to dinner. I convinced myself it had nothing to do with learning from Krish. He had arrived early in the morning and was catching up on sleep in the bedroom. I took it upon myself to test out and make sure each of the 300 Wizers he had carried were in working condition. It would take me a few hours, but we wanted no unnecessary surprises.

The batch of 300 were the first consignment out of an order for a thousand placed by the TAN Corporation. Krish and I had exclusive rights to use Wizers in the entertainment industry, and AYREE's supplier had produced the consignment in record time. There were a few enhancements. For one, the de-warping of the images from the FishEye lens was improved, and the black memory foam padding molded to the bridge of the wearer's nose for a snug fit. The cameras also had increased low light sensitivity. Krish awoke while I still had about a hundred Wizers left to check. "This is exhausting work."

"I told you they were checked by the QC department at AYREE," he said, "but of course go ahead, be a perfectionist. I've got something else I need to show you, mind if I log into the server?"

"Be my guest," I said, "and after you're done, come help with the backlog here."

I heard him work at the keyboard. At first it was distracting, hearing him tap tapping away. Then I got used to it as his fingers started playing the keys like a fine instrument. I was checking Wizers with the speed and efficiency of a well oiled assembly line by then. My phone alarm rang. He looked up.

"It's her rehearsal time" I said, "and I like to watch her

dance." I put on my Wizer.

Krish grabbed one I was testing from the floor and logged in. Maya was already by the window going through her moves.

"Lemme turn up the music a bit," I said and walked to the amp.

"What is this? It doesn't sound like the classical music she dances to," he said.

"Yeah, I know. She always said she wanted to experiment with mixing styles," I said. "I never understood what she meant until I listened to her collection." I pointed to the stack of dusty CDs on a rack near the amp. They were an assortment of jazz, ballet and Indian classical music that I had not paid attention to before.

"I mixed two of those tracks a few days ago and put it on the server," I recalled aloud. "Then on that day, as I watched her dance, something strange happened."

"What?" he asked, lifting his Wizer to his forehead.

"Put them back on. You'll see."

We watched Maya pirouette and then smoothly transition to the staccato foot tapping of Kathak. Kathak, looked to me like tap dancing. But where tap was more like a rock drummer taking off on a solo, Kathak sat more on the beat, rhythmic and percussive.

"Look at her!" he said. His mouth formed an O while his fingers came to the front of his lips.

"I know!" I said. "The mocap is bpm driven, so the only tweak I put in there was to splice the motion files and assign segments of them to a music style."

"You mean the music remix is triggering a swap of motion files on-the-fly?" he asked.

"Yes, to the style while conforming to the beat. I guess inverse kinematics is taking care of transitioning her body poses so no illegal or unnatural skeletal motions occur."

"That's what intelligent IK would do normally, yes," he said. "D'you know what this means for my research!"

For the next few minutes Krish and I forgot about all the work we had pending for the club launch. We sat on the floor watching Maya perform in her digital pointe shoes.

...

The day arrived. We were at Xanadu, Henry Tan's futuristic nightclub. Xanadu was going to be the first club where technology would be subtle and in-your-face. According to Henry, it would define the bar–and that was his pun–other clubs would be judged by. The club was full, as any opening night would be. It was a proper red carpet event, with the paparazzi vying for place, and flashes going off as celebrities walked in. The theme of the club was red and black. Space age, yet warm. Too many clubs went in for the cold steel and chrome look; not Xanadu. The bar-stools were upholstered in leather with black velvet trim, and they had a red embossed monogram "X" on the seat. All three bars, had black faux leather covered countertops with chrome footrests and Quad landing bays appropriately marked with an X.

There were eight Quads in service at the main bar and four at the bar on the higher level. A huge screen of cinema-like proportions formed the backdrop to the dance floor. Then there was the DJ cabin. It was more like a starship bridge. The lasers and James the DJ wearing a Wizer completed the command deck look. I walked up to the cabin, and he embraced me.

"Dude! Look at you. All millionaire and all," he said.

James was still good old James. He was a resident at Xanadu and manager of the club. Kelly looked gorgeous in black with her hair gelled down and a hint of red eye make-up. She was walking towards Krish and me balancing three flutes in her hand.

"To us!" she said.

"Where's Henry?" asked Krish.

I put my Wizer on and located him at the upper deck. He was looking down at the crowd. His Wizer was not on, so it was no sense sending a message that way. I sent via the screen instead: "To us, Henry!" He saw it flash and raised his glass. James stepped on the foot pedal and sent the fog machines into hyperdrive. I knew what was coming next. The dance floor throbbed with the industrial strength sub woofers. James was pumping adrenaline into the crowd. The lasers came on and scanned the smoke in a tunnel pattern, painting a red X call sign in the middle.

On James' insistence, four groove riders were installed around the perimeter of the dance floor. James had the bouncers make sure those foam saddles were reserved for female patrons only. That was James the manager. No one argued. He elbowed me and tilted his head in the direction of a brunette with her legs crossed tightly, knees together. She had the saddle horn in a vise grip between her thighs. James winked at me and triggered an LFE sample. She arched her back visibly and took a sip from her glass.

"Welcome to Xanadu." James' voice rumbled.

He put on his Wizer, and I knew he could instantly see the mesh of speakers arranged in an umbrella pattern. They were almost invisible to the naked eye in the darkened club ceiling. He gestured with his hand as if hurling a lightning bolt and sent a thunder clap sample to a group of speakers that were dead center over the dance floor. The infra red error correction enhanced software running the modified FishEye interpreted his gestures with millimeter accuracy. Five of the Quads took off from the bar and hovered over the dance floor.

On cue as the music rose to a crescendo, the Quads synchronized and tilted. Champagne rained on the crowd from bottles secured to the Quads.

There was a roar from the dance floor as people turned their heads to catch the drizzle of expensive rain that had been bottled a good many years ago. The Quads glided in formation over the floor, and as the music climaxed they flew off to their base stations at the bar. James was like a maestro, performing with his hands, panning music around the canopy of speakers overhead. He hurled a heavy rain sample at a ring of speakers as the Quads re-appeared and poured another round of champagne on the crowds. People were dancing surrounded by a sonic curtain of rain that could be heard only at the perimeter of the floor. I looked up at Henry. He was being applauded and patted on the back by his associates. It was then that I understood the secret to success of that astute businessman, Henry Tan.

Krish was talking to Kelly. Maybe something would work out there? I wished it would. The smile on his face suited him. I walked into the DJ Cabin.

"Just like old times, eh?" James said, offering me the turntables.

"Always nice to be back," I said. I lowered the pitch of the song being played in gradual increments until it matched the beat of the song that I had cued.

"If you've got your Wizers, wear them now. Or use your phones and connect to Xanadu net," I said on the mic.

I eased up the fader on the mixer, and the beat started. It was the same song that we had almost danced to on that fateful evening. All 300 Wizers were worn. People who didn't have one were watching through their phone cameras as Maya danced to the song on the stage under the projection screen. I plugged my Wizer's output into the club video system, and she came up on the big screen. A few people wearing Wizers climbed onstage to dance near her. The AI did a flawless job of detecting Wizers and phones close by. She drew back if someone danced too close, and they in turn realized and jumped back to give her room. The crowd on the floor gravitated toward her. They were moving to the music but their heads were turned to the performance on stage.

...

"It's complicated," I typed, changing the relationship status of my social network's profile page. I was at our table on the upper level of the club, when Krish came and sat beside me.

"Should I get you a drink?" he asked. "What you doing?"

"No, I'm good," I said. "Uploading her performance to the server and filling in the frame while it's fresh in my mind."

He smiled and looked over my shoulder.

"Is this weird, Krish? You know sometimes I don't know, I get confused." I was posting photos of Maya's performance to an album labeled "Memories with Maya."

"Three-hundred people wore Wizers today. At least another one thousand were logged in to the club's network. They saw her dance. They had a real experience," he said. "How can it be weird?"

"After someone's gone, it's only memories left behind for loved ones, Dan." He put his hands on my shoulders. "You found a way of making new memories with her. To me, nothing weird going on here."

I turned to look at him. Maybe it was the pure logic of a scientist's mind. Maybe it was the justification I wanted to hear no matter how illogical... whatever it was, that night Krish validated my beliefs, and I could never thank him enough. We walked to the velvet covered rail at the club and looked down at the dwindling crowd.

"Are you staying?" I asked, looking in the direction of Kelly who was sitting at Henry's table. "You can come home later any time."

"No," he said. "If you're leaving, I'm ready." He smiled. "Can we drop Kelly off on the way?"

"You sly dog," I said.

"Nothing like that. Just getting to know her," he said. We walked down the stairs, meeting Kelly halfway. She sidled up to Krish, putting her arm around his waist. "Everything was perfect. Daddy's really happy!"

Krish smiled. "Let's leave. I've a plane to catch. A.I.R.I's waiting on our signatures." As we made our way to the parking lot, Krish said, "Can we take 53rd?"

"That's the long way home," I said. "But yeah, why not?" We drove with the top down and I parked outside Kelly's building. Krish hopped out of the cramped backseat and opened the door for Kelly, extending his hand to help her out. I blew air kisses and watched the two of them walk to the building entrance. Krish hesitated then quickly leaned in for a quick peck on her lips. I flopped my head back, put the Wizer on, and looked up at the sky. Krish opened the door and jumped in. I straightened up, about to remove the Wizer when he said, "No. leave it on." He wore his too as I started the car and drove on.

We passed the skyscraper that I was working on in what seemed like ages ago. The cranes on the tower were not moving. The developers were not lying to me after all. My mind raced back to the day when I was on the footbridge with my phone camera. It was a good thing I had the Wizer on. He would not see my eyes welling up. I shifted the paddles on the steering wheel; I needed to get away as fast as I could. Krish sat upright from the sudden speed surge and clamped his hand on my shoulder. Only this time, it was to tell me to slow down. We passed the steps leading to the footbridge and to our favorite haunt; Copa Cabbana. I was about to make a turn when I heard her.

"I remember this place."

Her voice was clear yet almost a whisper in my ear.

I hit the brakes and swerved to the curb. I took the Wizer off and looked at him.

"Put it on, talk to her," he said. "Ask her what she remembers."

"What do you remember, Maya?"

"Those stairs...up to the Copa Cabbana. The first time we met."

"I'll never forget that day," I said. I looked at Krish. "Does this mean we can..?"

"Not exactly. She's really just cross referencing stored frames," he said. "I searched at home for Maya's voice recorder that had her recitals. The lab went through five plus hours of material to analyze her voice samples which they broke down to units of speech. It's not pitch perfect, but close enough." Krish stopped speaking for a moment. Then he said, "I'm working on getting Dad's voice too. The reason

I wanted you to drive by here, was to test if it would work."

I loosened my seat belt. I was still recovering from hearing Maya.

"I granted the AI access to the cameras on your Wizer," he said. "Remember when I told you about frames and how the AI could take snapshots of your environment, then run image and feature recognition?"

"Yeah..." was all I could manage.

"That's what just happened. The Wizer's sampling the real-world, extracting sensory cues... as everyone does, subconsciously."

"So, in effect... I'm Maya's Surrogate?"

"I suppose so. You could say you're her eyes, her ears... her sensory input." He looked at me and took his Wizer off. "Every time she looks through the Wizer, she's cross-referencing the present, to previously stored Frames, Memories."

I understood what he said, but at the same time questions started piling in my mind, like traffic backing up on a highway after an accident.

"Do you know what happens when people remember things?" he said. "The brain is always processing visual information. When it takes a snapshot of a location, and if something memorable has happened, like it did right now." He paused. "Days later, or even five years later, depending on the person, it will cross-reference those frames. The more time you spend sequentially recalling the contents and comparing it to the contents–or a trigger object–in a current frame, the more priority the stored frame will be allotted."

He looked at me, and realizing that he hadn't lost me yet, said, "You don't have to be physically present at a location for your brain to pull up older frames. You could jog your memory to recall them. What's important is how long you spend dwelling on the contents of one. That is the cue the brain uses when indexing or assigning priority, to a frame. It's what keeps a memory... alive. Connections are made and fired in the brain for all this to happen."

"Yeah, synapses." I said.

"That's right. What I'd like to think we've witnessed is the crude approximation of a synapse firing digitally–a Dynapse. He took a deep audible breath. "Of course this is a simplified and embellished explanation, but it's the premise my algorithms are based on. This doesn't mean the AI has gained consciousness. It just means that… Maya's learning to remember."

We sat in silence for what could have been a good few minutes. Finally, Krish took the Wizer off, sunk into his seat, and turned toward me. "Can we start the car now?" he said.

I exhaled and pulled back onto the road.

…

Krish had returned home and I was on my way to AYREE. They insisted that in keeping with protocol, I had to be there in person to sign official documents to cement our work relationship. I remembered my previous visit to Mumbai. Maya and Krish had been at the airport waiting for me. The familiar smells, the drive to the campus and as the car made its way up the driveway to the main campus building, all those memories came flooding back.

Krish and Prof. Kumar were waiting at the entrance as my car pulled up. It was an emotional reunion. We walked in to the lab and met with the rest of the team. I might have surprised Satish by giving him a bear hug, but he didn't know how much he had done for me. Neither could I ever tell him in words how much of a demigod he was to me.

Prof. Kumar was a board member. We took the elevator up to the main boardroom and met with the rest. The signing of documents was accompanied by handshakes and photographs. AYREE would have exclusive rights to use all existing IP that Krish and I had contributed in the field of homeland security and for the military. We retained the rights to use declassified IP and license it to other organizations for the entertainment and media industries. For any uses of the IP or the Wizer, we would go through AYREE. Krish was keen to explore solutions for medicine, therapy and rehabilitation. In addition to the agreed amount of one million two hundred thousand dollars, we would also be given shareholder benefits.

The Prof. invited us to his office to a celebratory lunch laid out for the lab team. After lunch he took Krish and me to his study; a glass partitioned area of his expansive office.

"What is it you wanted to show us, Krish?" said the Prof. after we were sitting. Krish stood up and walked to a chair.

"Put on your Wizers and run the update."

While we were running an update on the device, Krish said, "Run the threat assessment module."

The Prof. and I ran our fingers on Wizer's arm and double tapped it.

"You see how it's locked to the node on my wrist by default?" The yellow crosshairs are locked onto Krish's wrist as he grasped the chair back. Krish moved his hand behind the chair occluding his wrist. The crosshairs fluttered between his head and his shoulder. In a second, the cross hairs settled and locked onto his shoulder.

"Welcome to my algorithm, Code named, DHARMA-I."

"Unusual name," I said.

"It's a Sanskrit word, hard to translate," he said. "An example: Sugar's Dharma is to be sweet, Fire's Dharma is to be hot...that which is integral to something, might be a fair attempt at a translation."

"That's quite well put," said the Prof.

"You've heard of Asimov's three laws of Robotics? Well Dharma; my algorithm, has three times as many Ethics stops to make, prior to executing any routine. These laws are integral to the algorithm."

Krish folded his Wizer and pushed the chair back .

"I had to turn, in a way... to religion, to the ancient teachings of Sanathan Dharma, to build the DNA of my AI."

"The irony is not lost on me!" I said.

Prof. Kumar applauded. I joined in. "Well done Krish," said the Prof. He walked to the door and closed it. "Sit boys." he said. "Let me show you some near future plans we are looking at. These are recommendations I will be putting forward to the board, but as co-advisers, your input is valuable."

He went to a safe and unlocked it, taking out a transparent case and bringing it back to the desk. We leaned in to have a look. The object looked like a skin colored adhesive bandage. Only on closer inspection did we see the intricate circuitry printed on it.

"What is it?" I asked.

"All I can tell you now," he said, "is that it's a hybrid semiconductor and nanotechnology based design, and it allows us remote tactile sensing capability."

"Cyber Skin?" I said. My eyes must have widened, because he smiled.

"Even I don't know its true potential, nor understand exactly how it's created, but I do know we should investigate how it can be applied in projects such as DRONE."

"This is amazing," I said, "and it's all being done right here?"

"Not all," he said. "We work with other scientific research centers and share data. It's my job to see how these disparate technology advances can be brought together to put us ahead of others, while benefiting mankind at the same time," He was quick to close the lid of the box before he went on. "One thing I did ask the team was if it's possible to transmit the tactile data stream from such a patch of skin to a remote location."

"So our drones can feel?" Krish asked.

"Precisely. With a Quad we could theoretically maneuver

a simple armature equipped with a skin patch to send a remote feel-stream," the Prof. said. "At the control center, a glove covered with the same material and with sensors touching our skin could in theory reproduce the sensation electrically."

"Did they say it can be done?" I asked.

"Not yet, but it's something they can work on. Etching a wireless antenna for remote transmission of the data stream is possible in such a hybrid design."

"I think the board made a good choice in having you head AYREE, Prof," Krish said.

"I second that," I said.

"Thank you, boys, for the kind words," he said. "Here's some other plans which we have more direct control over and which I have recommended to the board."

Prof. Kumar's genuine enthusiasm showed as he rolled back his chair and opened and closed drawers, locking them shut, looking for the right one that had what he wanted to demo. In a moment of inspiration, he turned and went to the opposite wall and unlocked a cabinet. He took a file out and opened it in front of us. Each paper was watermarked "Classified." "This is a proposal to regulate and govern the ownership of Dirrogates," he said.

Krish and I looked at each other, and then we were listening.

"I see it, and I'm sure you both do as well, the immense opportunity there is in licensing Dirrogates to work overseas right at clients' premises. BPO two point zero like you've never seen," he said. "Our country is a huge business outsourcing destination. Why not have actual Dirrogates working at the client's facility where they can communicate with other human staff.

The Prof. leaned back in his chair, clasped his fingers over his head and looked up at the ceiling.

"Krish, as you've rightly pointed out, there will be many ethical and security issues to work out," he said. "I have yet to draw out complete plans, but I sent a brief feeler to the board members. I will, of course, need your co-operation and advice a hundred percent on this."

He walked back to the cabinet and returned with another file. "Here's another proposal to the board. It's for governing and releasing of geo coordinates of real world locations within the federal borders of the country for virtual worlds."

"Say goodbye to your lab in Ibiza." I said to Krish.

"Yes. I see it becoming a big issue if we do not look ahead on such matters," he said.

"Have you already presented this to the board?" Krish asked.

"I have. One of the members voted that I get this to the government," he said. " I think she may have a point! It's about time intellectuals, academia and scientists get involved in the governing of this fine land."

"Professor, you have my vote on both counts," Krish said, "on you joining a party and on wanting to usher in change."

"I don't get to vote here," I said, "but, you'd have mine."

“I discussed this with my family, and they are all for it,” he said. “I know there will be far less egos and petty bickering if we had more thinkers making policies and governing. We'd certainly have more rational arguments and discourse than what I see on TV, now.” It was the first time I saw a hearty smile on Professor Kumar's face.

“Well, boys, you've given me much needed votes of confidence. He rose from his desk. “Welcome aboard. Let's have a drink to our partnership. Sorry, I can only offer you tea or coffee at the moment.”

“Actually, I'd love to have a double of the cardamom tea,” I said, “I kinda missed it the most.”

We left his office and walked to the lab for a steaming cup. The car was waiting for us when we reached the main door of the building.

“Daniel, your apartment in the guesthouse is open for you,” the Prof. said. “In fact if you like we can have it permanently blocked for you, seeing how you might be here more often?”

“Thank you, Professor,” I said. “I love the offer, but tonight I'm booked at a hotel close to the airport. I would like to make a brief stop at the guesthouse, though, for old times sake.”

Professor Kumar saw us to the main door of the campus and bid us goodbye. The driver took us to the guesthouse. I got out of the car and Ram bhai was there, beaming.

“You've come back to visit, Daniel sir!”

“Just passing through, Ram bhai.” We shook hands for a

good minute or so. "Hang on a sec. I have something for you." I went to the boot of the car and opened my suitcase.

"Oh! Thank you so much, Daniel sir," he said.

He had once commented on how cool my backpack looked. I made sure I carried one for him.

Ram bhai lead us up the stairs and paused on the landing to search his large ring of keys. He unlocked the door to a part of my life which seemed so long ago. I looked at the dining table where we ate Indian food, the bedroom and the chair on which Maya had sat. Then I opened the glass door and the curtains caught the wind. We stepped out on the terrace and the white chaise longue was still there, with the bar table. The setting sun peeked through the trees. It was a day I remembered well.

Krish was behind me. He didn't say anything. He must have known I was reliving old memories. My backpack was on the dining table. I took out the FishEye and went to the storage room. There was a step ladder in there. Krish watched as I set up the FishEye near the glass door, aimed it out at the terrace and switched it on.

I got my Wizer and put it on. The compass on my smart phone showed me the reading of the location. I punched it in. The sun was shining low through the trees, lending a golden hue to the sheer white curtains.

"She's here?"

"Yes." I said.

Krish did not wear his.

He stood watching in silence, as I took pictures through

the Wizer. Maya looked beautiful. The sun brought out the highlights in her hair. It was well into dusk by the time we left the guesthouse. I said goodbye to Ram bhai and turned once again towards the green lawns of the campus when we pulled out from the gates.

As we passed Study Street, a peculiar sight caught my attention. I asked the driver to halt. Krish had a smile on his face. We got out of the car and crossed the street. Gathered in small groups under the cone of the phosphor and sulfur street lights were kids sitting cross legged on the pavement with slates in their hands.

Two boys looked up and waved at Krish. He acknowledged them.

"You did this?" I asked.

"Get your phone out and search for the network," he said.

"Logging into free network Study Street," I said.

"Correct," he said. "The network is restricted to educational Internet resources and online libraries."

He pointed to the top of one of the lampposts. I could see the wireless access point in there in weather proof housing. We walked down the street. There were more children with digital slates.

"Who paid for all this?" I asked.

"In a way, my dad," he said. "I'm continuing what he started. He always told me my intelligence was a gift from God, and I should use it to better the lives of people."

After a short silence I spoke. "For better or worse, regardless of my beliefs, I think he's right."

We reached another lamppost further down the street and he pointed up. "There's two FishEyes covering the entire street. You know the coordinates," he said. "Drop in sometime for a walk. We have so many things to teach these kids, and so many things to learn."

"I will," I said, "and that's a promise."

...

The flight left on time at six the next morning. I settled into my private pod on the A380 aircraft and wore my Wizer. The in-flight wireless network would be used to the max.

The aircraft was miles above the ground, and I was miles away from home. But in reality I was already with her. She was sitting on the couch with me, reliving memories we had made on that terrace. The A380 didn't have our song, but my home server did. My Dirrogate streamed it to me. The cabin lights dimmed. I took a sip from my glass and eased back into my pod. At home, we were moving to the beat of "Here with Me."

I was home. I entered the apartment and wore my Wizer. My Dirrogate dissolved. I wore the glove with the blue LED and reached out my hand to Maya. She reached out with hers, our fingers barely touching. She caressed her cheek. The glove hummed to life. I mimicked her move, closing my eyes, feeling Maya's touch on my face. Maya smiled and walked toward the window. It was almost sunrise. My phone rang.

"Krish?... is everything alright?"

"Yes. Are you at home?" he said.

"I've just got in. What's up?"

"Have you checked your news feed?"

"No. Doing it now." I walked up to my laptop and logged in. The timeline on the social network site showed a video with a stream of comments. I clicked Play. The video came up on the projection screen. It was Maya dancing. Her routine from the opening night at Xanadu. At places, the video went into slow-motion, showing her transitioning from Kathak to a full blown fouette – flawlessly.

"I'm watching the video," I said to Krish.

"Did you read the comments below?"

I scrolled the screen and saw a series of comments from simple '+1s' to 'well done', 'amazing', flowing down in a threaded stream. I stopped at one that read: ' This is beautiful. Can we use this routine?' Then it struck me... If her choreography had motivated a person to post a comment, it meant Maya had influenced our world for the first time.

"Opening her own dance studio was her dream," said Krish.

"Is, her dream, Krish. Those hours of frustration she'd go through because of her leg," I put on the Wizer, looking at her. "She's managed to hack her destiny. I'm proud of her." Below the last comment, I typed: 'Beautiful'

"Beautiful. The video is... beautiful?" said Maya, her voice clear. I turned around and looked at her. "The video, yes. And... you."

She smiled at me. Krish smiled on the phone screen and disconnected. The Sun had risen. I walked out to the sundeck. I stood, elbows resting on the sundecks rail, looking out at the city. In a nearby apartment cluster, through a window, I saw a woman. Sliding my finger over the Wizer's arm zoomed in. The woman was wearing a Wizer. Her hand reached out to touch the face of a Dirrogate - A young man in military uniform. I smiled and my gaze traveled to a higher floor. A toddler was playing on the floor in a living room. An older, silver haired digital surrogate materialized and smiled down at the child. His hand reached out and touched the top of the toddlers head.

The sun was now up in the sky. I closed my eyes, held them shut for a second and then opened them. The moment captured, forever.

EPILOGUE

Winter Solstice 2012 was a day I remember well.
I remember it as the start of a new era. An era where time didn't matter anymore.
What use was time to those who'd soon achieve Digital Immortality?
Many moons passed since Maya's first perfect Kathak routine. At times, I'd wake up just to watch dance.
At times... I still do.

Author Note

Memories with Maya was first published in Feb 2013. This updated version should hopefully be with you by mid July, 2014. There are quite a few reasons for this update. The most important ones being: I'm writing a screenplay based on the book, and as the plot of the screenplay unfolded, I felt a need to share it with readers and fans of the story. The final screenplay might still have a twist, but for the most part, you are now up to speed!

Another reason for updating the story was, I'd gotten a lot of questions on why the sex was borderline graphic with an emphasis on sexuality in a hard sci-fi story. It's all about reading between the lines, and subtext. That was (still is) my intention. The epilogue is another example. The ground reality is we've become used to information and entertainment in bite -or- byte sized, chunks. While many 'got' the underlying story, there were those who skimmed through. So, to appeal to a wider audience, I've toned down scenes in a few of the chapters, and compressed the story further.

Sex is a physical manifestation of Touch. Touch transcends dialog. One of the quests in the story, is to explore the encoding- the encapsulation- of touch, of emotion... digitally. Humans are visually and physically expressive by nature. Through technology, most of our senses have been digitized. Evolving to digital beings is perhaps, our destiny. This story seeds ideas for that fascinating journey.

Memories with Maya, since it's publication last year, has gained a fair share of praise and critique. Some have also wondered why hard science is wrapped in passages of juvenile writing... The only answer I can come up with, is: Authenticity. There's also been a good amount of praise and kind words. I'd like to take a moment to thank everyone who took time to write a few words on the book's Amazon and Goodreads pages, as well as reviews written by esteemed personalities in publications. A select few quotes follow on the next page.

In researching the story, I traveled and visited numerous nightclubs, food-courts, coffee-shops and campuses where the late teen to 25s hangout, and I eavesdropped on conversations and mannerisms. I was fortunate to be able to travel to multiple cities spanning the West, the Middle-East and Southeast Asia. I've extrapolated from mental, and documented notes that I made while researching the story. All main characters in the story are under 27, living EDM fueled lifestyles, while charting their future... similar to real people I observed in metropolitan cities.

A few words on the tech and AI... I aimed to keep the story as grounded in hard-scifi as possible, with what I think will be the state of the tech for the next decade, from prosthetics to AI. While I was tempted to throw in copious amounts of fantasy related to AI, as some recent Hollywood films have, I felt scenarios depicted in those films were non reachable in the coming decade.

"Dirrogates" and Memories with Maya is an evolving story... this is the beginning!

Thank you for reading.
Clyde DeSouza.

Praise for Memories with Maya

"In Memories with Maya, human sexuality gets an upgrade..."- ***iO9.com***

"AI and Augmented Reality add to the transhuman mix..." - **John Havens in Mashable.**

"He pulls an epic amount of research into his storyline on augmented eyeglass technology..."-***Ann Reynolds, in The Huffington Post.***

"I found the writing worked well for me. The pace was good, the prose was good." - ***David Brandt, HardSF.org***

"the 'Wizer,' an AR, see-through visor driven by AGI (artificial general intelligence) [is] Google Glass on steroids..." - **Giulio Prisco, Kurzweil A.I.**

"Just as I was, you will find yourself totally absorbed in the adrenaline rush of developing cutting edge technology..." - ***Jeff Wallace, Examiner.com***

"Sharp, high-tech sci-fi thriller -- will the future really be like this?..." - ***kacunnin, Top 500 Amazon Vine Voice Reviewer.***

...

www.dirrogate.com

Printed in Great Britain
by Amazon

49189454R10121